Ellen van Neerven (b. 1990) is a writer of Mununjali and Dutch heritage. She belongs to the Yugambeh people of the Gold Coast and Scenic Rim. She won the David Unaipon Award – Unpublished Indigenous Writer in the 2013 Queensland Literary Awards for *Heat and Light*. Ellen's short fiction, poetry and memoir have been published in numerous publications, including *McSweeney's*, *Voiceworks* and *Mascara Literary Review*. She lives in Brisbane.

HEAT AND LIGHT

ELLEN VAN NEERVEN

UQP

First published 2014 by University of Queensland Press
PO Box 6042, St Lucia, Queensland 4067 Australia

www.uqp.com.au
uqp@uqp.uq.edu.au

Cover design/illustration by Josh Durham (Design by Committee)
Cover photograph by Arcady31/Bigstockphoto
Typeset in 11/15 pt Bembo by Post Pre-press Group, Brisbane
Printed in Australia by McPherson's Printing Group

Cataloguing-in-Publication data is available from the National Library
of Australia http://catalogue.nla.gov.au

ISBN
978 0 7022 53218 (pbk)
978 0 7022 52938 (pdf)
978 0 7022 52945 (epub)
978 0 7022 52952 (Kindle)

University of Queensland Press uses papers that are natural, renewable
and recyclable products made from wood grown in sustainable
forests. The logging and manufacturing processes conform to the
environmental regulations of the country of origin.

Contents

HEAT

Pearl

It was a slight, old woman in a pie shop off the highway that told me who my grandmother was. I barely saw her over the counter but she propped herself up with one foot on the skirting board and pointed at me accusingly.

'You're a Kresinger,' she spat. 'I have something for you.' She tried to put what looked like a wood whistle in my palm. 'This was your grandmother's. She worked here.'

'No,' I said. 'My grandmother was Marie. Passed now, but she's my grandmother.'

'Sister,' the woman behind the counter said. 'That was your grandmother's sister.' She told me a story, starting with my grandmother's real name, Pearl.

~

The first time Pearl Kresinger was taken by the wind we were both twelve. It had been raining so long the water reached the library of our school on the hill. But it was the wind, cyclonic, that kept anyone with common sense inside. Not Pearl. She went out on the beach. She was standing on the jetty star-posed and everyone saw her. She seemed to fight with the wind for a moment, her torso wrenched back and her chin to the sky, but then we saw her fall into the grey water.

3

Trying to save her, one man yelled out he had felt her skin. But in the next wave he was gone.

A day later she came out with her hair streaked white, and the wind had settled. She didn't stay at school, none of them did, though I tracked her over the years.

Her skin was burnt butter, her forehead small and high, her fingers straight, her nails blue-grey from a permanent chill. She wore a red floral dress that dropped off her narrow shoulders. Her now black and white hair was waxy and feather-like, stretching down her back and creeping from behind her ears into her mouth when she turned to you. I could tell what others couldn't, her ears weren't really there, her eyes hissed and some of her teeth were missing. But the men followed the dance of her hair from back to mouth.

When the wind was kicking in and I'd be walking home from school near the beach through empty car parks, before the streetlights turned on, I'd see her between buildings, her hair entwined, her face in someone's neck, a man mostly, though there were women. It seemed all were hopeless against her.

After school I moved across the border and off the coast to a stopover town and got a quiet job behind the counter serving truckies.

I heard about the freak storm in the early fifties, Pearl Kresinger cheating death for the second time. The wind ripped the Kresinger tent up, into a tree. The others ran for shelter and Pearl stood there and let it lift her, she went into the electricity wires and they curled into each other like lovers as she was jolted. Her brother moved to her lifeless body and she touched him, and he took her place.

The people of the town drove her out of there. Nobody would touch her again. She lived in the hills for a while, and then she came to my town, and into my store.

I was jealous at the sight of her. The truckies passing through the store did not know of her curse.

It wasn't just that she was Bundjalung that made them think she was beautiful. It was the way she duck-called.

~

I tug at the traffic all the way back to the city, and quickly go into the house I grew up in. I find my father – on the back stairs, painting – who denies everything the old lady has told me. He spills paint three times on his boot, so I know I have to go back.

My thoughts are running wild as I drive to my place. If I didn't know my grandmother, then how could I know myself? My grandmother as I had always known was Marie Kresinger, Aunty Marie to everyone. She'd spent most of her life as a domestic. She died from heart failure at the age of seventy-two. People said her heart was too big. I was eleven. My dad wanted me to sing an old-time song at the funeral but I was too shy.

She was the daughter of Zahny Zahny, otherwise known as Jack Zahn Kresinger. He was one of the men the settlers gave the title of King of his people. Zahny Zahny had three wives and ten children; Marie had many half-sisters and brothers, and maybe I had heard the name of one of her sisters, Pearl, in passing. Grandmother Marie wasn't here to tell her own story, and my father would tell me nothing about our history, whether he knew it or not. This leaves me with the shopkeeper. It is Sunday afternoon, after closing time. I will have to go back down the freeway tomorrow, to the pit-stop just over the border.

I grip the wheel to hear my thoughts. I am Amy Kresinger, twenty-six and already war-weary with life, already feeling pushed into the ground like some sedated potplant.

The usual reason I go down the highway and to ancestral country is to go surfing, not to meet family or do any of the practices you'd expect me to do.

I thought I was going to become a nice woman one day, get married, have a cosy family, and be called Aunty, all because of my grandmother Marie. I thought I'd mellow and tame with time. Now I'm not so sure.

When I arrive back at Jimmy's Pies the old woman is rolling up the doors, no one beside her. This old woman can spin a yarn. She puts her whole body in it.

~

There is a kind of woman that draws men like cards, that has beauty, and knowledge as well in those siren eyes. That's Pearl Kresinger. Jimmy hired her before she even opened her mouth. She was put in the kitchen with him. He said every morning, 6 a.m. It didn't feel kosher, at that time, in the sixties, to have a black woman working at your establishment. That's why Jimmy put her in the kitchen, I assumed, though she wasn't out of sight. When the pies were in the oven baking, she was out there on the tables.

I don't know where she learnt to duck-call. Women don't duck-call, at least not where I'm from.

There were three men who usually came in most mornings around eleven. They'd shot a few thousand roos, rabbits and camels between them, but what they all had in common was the ducks. One of the men had lost sight in one eye. They called him Bandit for his eye-patch. I'd heard he was in a highway crash when he was younger. Two roos went through the windshield.

I was behind the counter half the time and swept the floors and ran errands for Jimmy the rest. I melded in – I was invisible when they wanted me to be.

The shop was a brothel before they made the highway. Then it was a warehouse for sporting goods. Jimmy had bought the place and done it up a year before I'd started. The cars were starting to pull in, most came from trips to and from Brisbane, which was really starting to boom.

Jimmy liked that Pearl was strong – she could carry the boxes of meat from the delivery. He was getting on, his strength was starting to decline. And compared to Pearl, I was a Chihuahua.

Although Jimmy and Pearl started before me every day, they did most of their work in the afternoons. Pearl was getting good at cutting the pastry, learning the techniques. Sometimes I watched her from where I was standing and although I already felt a strong sense of responsibility and ownership of the store in what I did, I wished I was the one making the pies.

Pearl snapped the scissors when she was bored, which was often. One time we were alone and I said to her, 'Do you remember me from school?' She didn't answer.

The truckies loved meat, and they loved our pies. I was sitting behind the counter when Bandit's group came in. These three men played long games of dice as they sat there, bludging, until mid-afternoon. I listened and heard the gossip of the surrounding towns where they lived. They requested I play anything but the Bee Gees on our tiny wireless, perched on top of the glass cabinet.

The other two were opposites: Goh was a tall thin skeleton of a man, married and silent. George was fat, and the one who talked the most. Between the three of them, they mainly discussed the road, hunting and women. Jimmy would come out and talk with them. They were ex-crims, the lot of them.

The truckies were the kind of men who talk about hating native women. There was a lot around here, and Jimmy told Pearl it would be best for her not to come out while they were there.

'Bad men,' Jimmy said to her. 'But they're half my business.'

Pearl didn't listen, of course, and one day when they were talking about wildfowl she went out and sat down at their table. They looked at Pearl as if she was possessed. They were dazzled by her stories, and of course the flash of pale on her brown body, her well-positioned cleavage.

The men didn't look at me. I was just a short woman. Pearl and I were the same age, going on thirty, though she trumped me in conversation. No one looked at me twice, I was big-eared, pale and freckled.

Pearl bragged about catching ducks, even said we should start selling duck pies here. The men were dim, they didn't see her for what she was.

~

I am like my grandmother Pearl. I am a strong black woman, and love comes too easy for me. There is always someone to drown. I have those Bundjalung eyes, too.

My father doesn't know that I go to those coffee shops in the inner-west, where the older, wealthy women go, women who like women.

It is always a bit of an intellectual seduction. I offer to buy them a cuppa, ask them what they're reading. Women like that are always reading. Searching for women like them in the texts. True they're always keen, their hand movements on the tabletop say it.

Today I snare Shirley. I've been meeting her for months now, on and off. She has a long-term partner, ten years or more. Shirley is gorgeous. She is in her forties but looks thirty. Blond curls, surfer looks. A dazzling smile. Strong, masculine hands. Nails cut.

This time I meet her at the pub for lunch in the industrial section – this shows I mean business. She is sitting there when I rock up. She always wears a sports jacket even if it's humid outside. And flash jeans that are tight at the crotch. When we finish our meal and drinks I get her to follow me along the road, under the freeway, where the milk factory is. It is 3 p.m. on a Friday and we are around the corner and out of sight of the state post office and the Murri art studio. We're by the fence. I cup her small angled face and she grabs my collar as we kiss, our crotches already pressing together. Her jeans are easy to undo and I slip my hand in that small gap between her underwear and the hot centre of her. She groans like I knew she would and she roughly palms up my skirt, pulls my thong down to my knees. I lift up the hem of the skirt and pull her to me. We give up on kissing. A train vibrates the tracks above us, and the shudder goes to the ground.

Driving home I switch on the radio and one of those old Motown voices comes on and reaches my heart. I have a boyfriend. He's a teacher. When I first met him I thought I could marry him. Now I say I'm too busy to meet on weekends and he should be catching up on his marking. I don't want to be the person who captures the hearts of many.

I am often stirred by a woman walking down the street or at a bus stop. In my teens, I was one of the ones every Friday night in the last carriage on the 1 a.m. train having sex with anyone who would have me. I am cursed to be this.

I remember the next half of the story the old woman told me.

~

Pearl Kresinger had only been in town for a week or two but she was already known for her duck calls, people in town had seen her by the waterways. She always wore her call around her neck, between her breasts, so the men couldn't help but notice it.

Goh, Bandit and George were obsessed with wildfowl hunting, a distraction from their meandering lives. Individually they were hopeless, but as a group they got some luck, they weren't too bad. They talked of the Pacific blacks and the hardheads.

'What do you go after?' Bandit asked Pearl.

'The mallards,' she said, surprising them.

'How many?' Goh asked.

'Fifteen, once. Or more.'

There was a silence. Standing there, behind the counter, I knew they'd never shot that many in their life. Bandit seemed to make a decision. He pointed to the wood whistle around her neck. 'Show us.'

She tugged at the string and brought it to her lips. It was a noise that sounded nothing like her voice – an immersive murmur that carried across the shop and lasted a total of four seconds. I was holding my breath and I didn't know why. Her body, her thick brown arms seemed to shine into a bronze and the men couldn't keep their eyes off her.

I wished I had an excuse to go outside and not watch them inflate with her. I could go to the car park and stand looking at the cars and maybe have one of Jimmy's cigarettes, even though I hadn't smoked in years.

In their thick silence, the men were in agreeance that they couldn't replicate such a natural vocalisation.

'You should come out with us sometime,' Bandit said.

'You'd be our little luck charm,' George said, wiggling his fingers.

Pearl played with her lips, 'But I got no gun.'

'We do.'

She twirled her hair, and I saw the different bits of colour, the streaks of deep white, the etch of electricity.

'Show us again,' Bandit said firmly.

They made her draw the call until her eyes teared up.

Bandit said, 'You reckon fifteen. You're going to have to prove it.'

~

I carried a special sort of shame from not singing at my grandmother's funeral. Everyone said Aunty Marie was a classy sort of woman; in photos, she was always looking

11

flash in opals and her hair all up and everything. I know I come from a different era, but dressing up for me is leaving the thongs at home and collapsing my ponytail.

I initially rejected the thought of Pearl being my grand-mother. What the woman at the pie shop had said about her made her sound like a succubus, cursed, a monster. I wanted eventually to be the baking biscuits type, like Aunty Marie; I honestly believed I would get there one day. I told my father and the other mob at the youth centre I outgrew singing, like it was a pair of shoes. But I do sing to myself sometimes, when I can't go to sleep.

Marie Kresinger had two children older than my father, a boy and a girl. She was raising them out at Hune Hill, on the family's property, when Pearl must have come to see her with news of her pregnancy. Their father had recently passed and Marie, her husband and the kids had moved back into the house at Hune Hill after living in Brisbane. Marie had been living in Brisbane ever since she'd married at the age of eighteen.

I have one photo of my great-grandfather. He has long hair in his face. In a photo taken at the mission, he sits on the right. They had put the king plate across his neck. I wondered if he had got used to the weight, the way it clanged to his chest when he walked.

He had made friends with one of the whitefellas high up, Malcolm, who recognised him as an important man among his people, this helped out the family quite a bit. My great-grandfather would bring mob together at this Malcolm's place and they would sing. All English songs. Malcolm taught my great-grandfather to read over one summer and so he was keen to show his favourite daughter, Marie, when he went to visit her in Brisbane.

I have been told the story a number of times of my great-grandfather walking alongside the road on his way to the town, when Malcolm's car pulled up alongside him. Malcolm stuck his head out of the car and asked, 'Where you going, mate?'

'See my daughter.'

'We got the new track, mate. I'll get you on. Lot faster.'

The railway was spanking new, and it glistened in the sun. He stepped on the train. Wind in his hair. A free pass was unheard of. Though this was the last time he took it up. The next few years, while he could still walk, Zahny Zahny was known for walking along the railway lines, not catching the train.

Marie and Pearl were the closest in age, and were like salt and pepper shakers, opposites, but always together. Zahny Zahny tried not to show it, but they were his favourite daughters. When the children were growing up he made sure they knew certain things. In spring, stone-grey seeds floated in the breeze and spread across the reddened dirt. He told his daughters not to pick up the seeds. Those who could not understand would say that they were dispersed by the wind man.

~

One cloudy day when Jimmy wasn't around the men called Pearl out of the back. 'Let's go out to the lake,' they said. 'A good day for it, ducks like getting wet.'

The lake was a dark place in town folklore, a sinkhole for small children and women. A euphemism for many things. I'd heard from their conversations that the wildfowl flew more on cloudy or rainy days, even though Goh liked the visibility of the sunny days.

They told Pearl she had to come along, 'We'll wait until you finish here. Right outside. Bring your gear and we'll walk down.'

Pearl's dress was a warm orange-red with a geometric print. It must have been new. The group finished their pies and walked out as early as I'd ever seen them do. It was only 12 p.m. Three hours until knock-off. I wondered what Pearl was going to do until then.

When they were out of sight, Pearl turned to me and acknowledged me for the first time. 'Can you come?'

I blinked for a few moments. She continued to stare at me with her dull eyes. That's when I knew what was going to happen explicitly. They were going to take her there, away from the protection of the store and Jimmy and they were going to attack her. And I would be there to know it.

~

After I talked that last time to the shopkeeper, I shot straight through, kept going down the highway. I went to the family property near Casino, halfway between somewhere. *Hune Hill* is what the sign said. I remembered the house a little bit from staying there a few times when I was younger. Grandmother Marie lived there with my Aunty Irma and my cousin Colin.

At the front of the property was an assortment of wild dogs tied to trees, and old raggy goats. It was raining. Aunty Irma came out in her nightie and ushered me in. The rain only touched my boots. Aunty hadn't seen Colin, who now lived in Sydney, for as long as I hadn't, so she was happy to see me, and more than willing to tell me about my grandmothers.

Marie was very surprised when her sister came to her to tell her she was pregnant. From the curse, and all the years that had passed, she thought Pearl couldn't have children. She hadn't seen Pearl for a long time. Marie watched as Pearl's belly swelled and she walked the stairs of the house holding her back.

It had been understood from the very beginning that Marie would take the child. The baby, when it came, was ugly, huge, as if it had waited there, in Pearl's womb, all of her adulthood. Pearl left the baby boy, a few hours old, and Marie quickly learnt to hold it as if it was hers.

~

At 3 p.m. I looked out of the window to see the three men standing with bags by their boots. They were dressed in camouflage and looked slightly ridiculous considering the weather. Their waterproof pants made their legs look like parachutes. They looked at Pearl's bright dress.

'Why you wearing that?'

She shrugged.

'You dumb bitch, we'll see how you go.'

I followed them down the streets. I had the advantage of knowing the town and the paths very well. Pearl was in front. Goh coughed on occasion and Bandit smirked. I saw them look at each other and communicate a shared want they could not say out loud.

When they went into the bushland with their gear, the decoys they carried began to weigh them down and they walked slowly – all three were unfit or weak. Pearl carried nothing and walked easy. I noticed she had slipped off the clogs she wore at work and was barefoot.

When the lake was in sight I stopped to find a vantage point. I found the old wooden lookout that had been there since I was a kid and surveyed the surroundings below. The men stepped out and surveyed the area and where they would set up the blind. Pearl half-turned; her eyes found me and she nodded in recognition. The little flecks of light flicking up from the lake caught their expressions and I felt I could see them perfectly. The men crouched to set their plastic painted decoys down in the mud. From where I was, the decoys looked quite lifelike. Pearl had found her spot a little bit further down, closer to where I was. She also knelt and opened her hands, and I saw she had made a grass duck, out of reeds. It was beautiful.

Bandit looked – his mouth gaped for a moment and then he laughed at her creation. I couldn't help but share his sentiment, as remarkable as it was, there was only one.

They stepped back thirty metres or so into the vegetation and started to get their gear out of the bags. George handed Pearl a shotgun. 'Don't miss,' he said. And they put on their gloves and face masks, and held their calls and their guns. Pearl stood straight and stripped her dress off, spread out her arms and slipped off her undergarments.

'Shit,' George said and they exchanged a placating look between the three of them that made them carry on as if nothing had happened.

With her feet, Pearl covered the red garment with

leaves. Bandit gave a nod to indicate the start of their hunt and they widened their stance.

Pearl put the call in her mouth. The wind picked up and melded with her hail call, a long, low note. The wind began to pull at the tassels of the lake, and I held my hair in place. The wind shuddered the ten or so decoys the men had laid out, and they fell down in a row.

The men swore loudly but Pearl kept calling. She went to a new call – a rapid round of short, sharp notes. This is what the men in their conversations at the shop had called a feed call, when a hen has found food. I heard the ducks above, and I looked up to see their formation swooping down. The mallards slowed their wings and came towards the outstretched Pearl like a train to a station. There were at least two dozen. Pearl raised the gun and fired. But nothing was shot. The mallards landed unaffected around her. She looked down, confused, at the gun.

That's when the camouflaged men made their move. With their masks they looked like executioners and that's what they were. They grabbed Pearl by the shoulders. Goh on the left, George on the right and Bandit at the front.

I got to my feet but there was nothing I could do. Though the wind, as always, was on her side. The gale swept back – it was a wind that bit – and George let go. He flailed his arms out and toppled backwards into the lake.

In the confusion Pearl got away and then she was running and Bandit and Goh were chasing hard and I could not see everything exactly. The heat from the day had carved a dull headache in my mind.

~

On the way home I find a lover, in a hotel in a one-street country town. She smells like apricots and is too pure for me. I started surfing when I realised I needed something to quell my undiagnosed sex addiction. When I go out to the beach it's usually to clear my head from anyone muddled up in there. Mystery does not always equal desire, and for every woman I've been with there has been one who turned me down. Like that Fleetwood Mac song, women, they will come and they will go.

This woman doesn't turn me down. We giggle as we pay the clerk for a room upstairs. As she unlocks the door I search her hands for a ring or tattoo or some sort of sign that will remind me that she is not mine. She is the kind of girl I would have thought about being with when I was younger and hadn't yet fucked up a million times. She gardens and she volunteers at the school near Hund Hill where lots of my mob went. She says she will take me to see the farm where she lives and show me her orange trees. They are the biggest oranges, the size of basketballs and they taste like love.

'Will you cut them up for me?' I ask.

'Yes,' she says, slipping off her singlet top.

'And take the skin off?'

'Of course.'

We take the covers off the bed and she gently puts her hand on my chest and drives me back onto the mattress. She lowers herself and her legs come around my waist – I squeeze her ankles and we kiss like we've kissed each other before. How can it be that I don't feel the weight of her. That there is no taste on her tongue. No drug, no cigarette, alcohol or coffee. I thought she'd taste like apricots or oranges. I'm getting sick, it might be the flu I've resisted all winter. Because I can't continue. My breath is ragged and the shapes and colours of her are blurring.

~

I found Pearl lying on the ground a long way from the lake. She had called me there with her whistle. She looked half-dead.

The jealous part of me could have kept going but I helped her. I felt a bunch of guilt that I hadn't done anything. And I had been one of those who had talked about her at school, and after I finished school, I had helped in outcasting her. She had come here to the town for a fresh start and she hadn't got it. I got her up and walked her to the lookout where I know she stayed for a time.

~

So much is in what we make of things. The stories we construct about our place in our families are essential to our lives. My father still won't say anything about it. He refuses to admit that Pearl is his mother. I make him have a break from the painting and sit him down at the kitchen table and try to convince him to accept the truth. I guess he doesn't want to know that his mother didn't want him, and all of the other things she was. But I think she was a fighter. I think there is a lot of struggle in our family and she has passed on that strength. I don't know yet if she's alive or dead, at peace or not, but I know she deserves to be a part of our family's history. The woman at the pie shop left me with this last piece of information.

~

The next day when I turned up for work I heard that the bodies of all three men were found. All three of them had heart attacks, but somehow they linked it to Pearl. More rumours began to circle around the traps, about her shame and how when she was young the wind man had taken her ability to have children.

It was a few years until I figured it out. She had transferred the curse to me, by blowing the spores into the whistle and calling me with it.

I don't get people wrong. I knew she was trouble.

~

I feel the old woman's fury ripple through me. And then I look at the wooden call in my palm. There's a tiny grey spore sticking to my finger. The old woman had done it. She had cursed me back.

Soil

Amy Kresinger leant back in her chair – with one hand to her temple and the other clutching the phone at a little distance away – and said her first words of the conversation, 'I don't want to talk about Colin.'

She said so in a final, reasoned way that she thought might sway her father away, but he was an ex-Navy officer who in retirement read Russian spy novels by the dozen, a skilled, primed negotiator.

'Please, Amy. Just put it to the board,' he said in a soft tone reserved just for a father with a daughter as his only child. 'At the next meeting, please.'

Amy ran the ATSI Youth Development Centre in Chermside. She said, 'He can go somewhere else. There's more places.'

She shouldn't have answered the phone. She was on holiday in Maleny. She had a nice room looking out into the hinterland. The only sound she'd heard outside this morning had been finches and honeyeaters.

The woman who ran the bed and breakfast had looked at her funny, like they always did, when it was just her and she didn't have a kid in the back seat. Though she seemed nice and helpful and kept out of Amy's way. She let Amy know of the spa outside, and how to fill in the breakfast sheet.

Her dad was still talking and she felt her stomach coil. 'We haven't even seen him, Dad. It's been twenty years,' Amy said, tapping her feet in frustration. 'He doesn't identify.'

Colin had been living in Sydney ever since he left to go to university. Amy thought about what must happen when Colin was at a bus stop and someone called out, seeing the Bundjalung in him, do you have any smokes, bruz? Colin would probably look the other way, smooth his suit. Now that she'd thought about it, it was likely he didn't even catch the bus, it would be beneath him.

She didn't know why Colin had come up out of nowhere all of a sudden. The forms had been sent through by email. Colin's mum, Aunty Irma, had been on the phone to Amy's dad, Charlie. Amy had immediately thought Colin probably just wanted to get the housing loan.

Her father said, 'Why won't you help your brother–cousin, Amy?'

'Don't do that to me, Dad.' She sighed.

Her father had gone all sentimental in his old age. 'Just because they've gone away. It's our job to bring them back.'

As president she had made strict rules about who she accepted, it wasn't just anyone. They must know who they are and they must be living as who they are. With those whose applications were rejected, she didn't use the terms that some of the others did, 'coconut', and so forth. She understood it was easy for some of their mob to be white and project a whiteness. She imagined it was easy for them to live out their lives this way. And one day it might click, when they needed a job, a house, a surgery. Too easy. I'll be black now.

The people in the Murri unit might say, 'Where you from? Haven't seen you around.'

He might stumble out a family name or a language group or vaguely describe an area that had some significance in an earlier life. He'd pray they didn't see right through.

When she got off the phone she felt an upsurge of guilt and pulled at her cheek. Her father had succeeded in tripping her up about it.

They weren't blood cousins. She had found out later in life they didn't share the same grandmother. Her grandmother had killed her own brother by electrocution. That was what they did to each other in her family, she guessed.

Amy and Colin got along well as children. He had grown up on country in the family house. She remembered the magnificent view, and how healing the air felt against her skin when she went there. Aunty Irma and her dad bickered constantly. He'd come over and fix the fence and the plumbing, and say, when are you going to get a new man? Aunty would flush and look sideways at Colin. Colin's dad wasn't in the picture. Amy's mother died when she was nine and her dad had never tried to get a new woman.

As a kid, Amy had thought about her and her dad going to live with them – Aunty, Nana and Colin. But they started going there less and less when Colin turned foul as a teenager, and Nana passed away.

Now Colin was married with four children and worked as a high-school teacher. Of course they would live in the eastern suburbs, and drive a Pajero, and his kids would go to one of those schools that had never even seen a child who wasn't white.

Amy stepped outside into the cool of the veranda and felt the bugs probing her sides. She was here in the cabin for two more nights. There were the markets and the shops and the cafes but she would be happy not to leave the accommodation.

She had got her dad off the line by saying, 'Okay, Colin can call me.' She'd admit she felt a pleasurable sort of anticipation at the thought of speaking with him. She imagined his unsure, surprised voice. She would tell him off real good, but she'd do it a clever way.

She met up with Colin in Sydney, one time, a lot of years ago, before he had the kids. She was there on a leadership conference. He had a girlfriend, she wasn't sure if this was the one he'd ended up marrying or not, she hadn't received a wedding invitation. Colin told Amy he'd take her out to dinner, with his girlfriend and his girlfriend's brother. They'd gone to KFC. That was Colin, always cheap.

He'd told a story, perhaps it was to impress the brother. A racist joke, like one from the comments you see on Yahoo news. Amy had always thought they'd come from bored rednecks in country Queensland. Not from her own flesh and blood. It wasn't even a good joke.

She was too shocked to speak before he got up and went to the counter to get another drink. She looked at the faces of the girlfriend and the brother, who looked completely pacified. They had planned to walk around Darling Harbour after dinner but she said she wanted to have an early one as she had to present the next day. That was it. The last time she talked to him. They were well into their forties now.

She saw a green tree snake glide along the path, its tongue flicking back and forth. She walked closer, observing its shiny skin. She'd always liked snakes, ever since she was a kid. Colin couldn't stand them, even though he was the one who grew up out bush. She'd scared the shit out of him one Christmas, dangling a carpet python around her neck.

A few hours later, when she was fixing something for dinner, her phone rang. Unknown number. She picked it up.

'It's Colin,' he said. He sounded very far away. 'How are you?'

She held herself. 'Not too bad.'

They were saying goodnight to their kids. 'Sorry about that,' he said.

'No, that's okay. What's your wife's name again?'

'Kylie.'

'Tell Kylie I said hi.'

There was an awkward pause, and then she decided to continue. She told him what she had told her father and the other members of the board at the centre.

'Really?' he said. 'But I'm your cousin.'

'It doesn't matter, Colin.'

Another silence before he said, 'I get it. What can I do?'

She hesitated. She had expected anger, not complacency.

'You come back up this way for a few days. You meet with us. You bring your family. You see the old mob, too. You listen to them. You do this three times and we'll see.'

He surprised her by saying, 'Okay.' There was a disturbance on the line. 'We're not children anymore,' he said.

'Yes, Col,' she said. The childhood nickname, spilling out like oil. She wondered if he thought she had changed from the fourteen-year-old girl he had known so well. She wondered if he was disappointed in her, as she was in him.

He continued. 'We have either succeeded or failed in getting over the horrors of our childhood.'

When she got off the phone she went back inside and got the breakfast card and the pen off the table and walked back out to the tree-flanked path. She thought she'd have the corn fritters and one piece of fruit, or maybe two. And the eggs, runny, with bacon and tomato. No bread. And what the heck, she'd have yoghurt and muesli, too. Drinks: how about a juice, but not just any juice, a pineapple one, and white coffee and black tea, but she'll write a little note to bring the coffee out first.

Her father was a well-respected man, and his name had built a lot of her. He would most likely get his way, like he always did. She could see, she would give in: Colin would eventually get that seal off the board to use for good or bad. She hadn't even asked him what he needed it for.

She saw the tree snake was no longer there. It must have moved while she was in her head. It had gone back to what was there, bark and leaves, the unfixed remainders of the ancient trees. If they were all remainders, how could they be picked apart from each other?

Hot Stones

Thirteen is the age that makes you. I lived in the Hill End Road house with my mother and grandmother. When I complained about no electricity, or that the toilet was outdoors, my grandmother said, 'Colin, look,' pointing to the grasslands that surrounded our property and the mountain they held. 'You are living and breathing on country. This makes you my very special grandson.'

When dinner had been prepared and I'd eaten with my usual ferocity, I would sit eagerly by my grandmother's side and wait for her yarnin' time. Even when I could barely keep my eyes open, I put my head to the floorboards and listened.

As the only child in the house, I liked when my cousin Amy came to visit with my uncle, and we would nick the quad bikes at the car shop on the corner and race through the flats. The bikes never had much fuel, so we knew we could only go so far – our perimeter was the most-times empty creek bed or Magpie Rock.

I knew we were both itching to go further, knowing that when we got home, Amy would have to go before dusk, back to the city, and I would be thinking about school the next day.

School and the other kids was still something I was

negotiating. My father had come from Ireland so I wasn't very dark. When I passionately shared a few of the stories my grandmother told me, the other kids called me half-caste. It didn't really stop me, though; I even spoke up in English class, because the teacher was talking like we weren't even here before, and I got kicked out and had the whole oval to myself until lunchtime. I made a nest out of the twigs. I was the sort of kid who couldn't stop touching the earth, sculpting it with my hands.

That was when I saw Mia. She was beautifully brown. Her face was brown and her arms were brown and her legs were brown. She was walking with her adoptive mother – they had come through the gate at the bottom of the oval. I gathered up my bottle caps and put them in the pockets of my shorts and scrambled over the banks and followed them. I knew I should have made myself known and helped them find their way, but I straightaway felt embarrassed that I wasn't in class. They would smell the cigarettes on my breath and think I was a delinquent. Plus Mia was dressed all pretty, too, shiny black shoes and white socks. Too flash for us Murris here.

They disappeared into the school office. After lunch I saw she was in my class. I rushed home and told grand-mother, 'There is another black kid in my class! A girl!'

Grandmother said, 'Go easy. I have to see if we're related, first.'

Mia had come from up north way. I talked with her and found she tolerated my humour. I shared with her half of the biscuit that my mother packed me.

While we were sitting under a tree I felt a sharp sting on my leg and said I'd been bitten. 'Probably a spider or something,' I said, rubbing the red mark on my knee. She looked down at my leg and laughed. 'That's an ant bite.'

We hung out after school. I took her to see the places I took my cousin, and we found our own places, too.

One of these places was the small steep hill near our property. It crawled with a sort of shrub and was a challenge to climb. Mia was new to the terrain, and often stopped to touch the leaves of certain trees. I was used to her slowing us down. She pulled one of the dry vines out from under the small plant. The plant had little round berries, the colour of bush tomatoes, except they were fuzzy.

'These look like what we have at home,' Mia said. She was excited by it. 'The old women, they told me about it. They use it for bush medicine.'

'For what?' I asked.

'Headaches, toothaches, all kinds of things. When a girl has her period, too.'

I blushed for some reason and even got my shoelaces caught.

I noticed that Mia liked to draw in class. When the two-week anniversary of our meeting came around I got her a book – *The Art of Drawing Trees* – from the flea market at the showgrounds.

I'd say I was in love. My heart burned and my stomach dropped into my pants.

She was ballsy and she was fast. We raced each other. Her legs were like stalks – and she had the skinny Murri ankles. She beat me still.

29

She came home with me most afternoons, when we were tired and hungry. We sat on the floor drinking ginger beer and I was in bliss having all my favourite people around me. Mum and Nana loved her as much as I did.

Mum and Nana were in the kitchen cooking chicken. Knowing dinner was a long way off still, Mia and I were planning the route for a race. It was going to be from the creek to Magpie Rock. Mia felt for the dusty curtains behind her and put her head outside; her nose twitched.

'Is it going to storm?' she asked when we stepped outside.

One side of the sky was blue and the other was black, so it could go either way.

'Don't wait 'til the migar n maral' my grandmother would say to me. 'Don't wait until the thunder and lightning.'

Mia was wincing at the first sign of moisture dropping from above.

I goaded her. 'You scared?'

She gave me a hurt look, and mumbled something about having to get home. She disappeared into the darkness. And even though I would see her again the next day, I was devastated and I went to bed cradling her scent. The storm didn't even hit.

What I didn't get was how the other kids treated her at school. Where they treated me with an acceptance sharpened by a respectful weariness, every class was built as a game around laughing at her. Mick Hammer called her names I didn't quite yet understand. And Mick's likely girlfriend, Emily (it wasn't official yet), said she was dog ugly.

Mia was still herself in class and Mum would say to her, 'They're just jealous of your looks, bub.'

Mia didn't talk of the family that she might have had and might have known. She loved her guardian, though Mia said she was always telling her not to do things. Mia would imitate her to a tee; 'Mi, speak English! Mi, don't swear, Mi put your shoes on, Mi don't eat that.'

One day Emily came to school unable to talk because of a toothache. She was struggling with it and she would have to wait 'til the weekend to go to the dentist.

Mick held her hand as if she was dying. When they walked from class to class everyone stared at the way she held her mouth like it might fall off. On the third day of this, Mick said, 'Can anyone help her?' My mother was a nurse before she raised me, and the women in town often called her up to ask her things, but there was no way I was going to help Emily.

Mia surprised me with her benevolence when she whispered, 'Those berries we saw on the hill, Colin.'

Mia went back there without me and got a handful of the berries off the tree. The next day she walked up to Emily on the playground. Emily looked at her suspiciously. Emily was the one that had started the trend for all the girls in our grade to not go within ten metres of Mia, and walk fast when walking past her, which meant that Mia was always by herself when the girls and boys were split up. If one of the girls forgot, Emily would snort her horse-like giggle and say, 'Oh, you got fleas now.'

Emily must have had the toothache so bad because when Mia said, 'Here, put these in your mouth, they will help. Don't swallow,' Emily looked left and right and accepted them in her hand. When Mia lingered, Emily opened her nasty mouth and said, 'What are you looking at, dog? Get away from me.'

I took Mia away and said, 'Why did you help her?' Mia just shook her head.

Before the next class, I went to have a smoke in the out-of-bounds area behind the stand-up shacks. Mia, like always, refused to come when I went for a smoke.

When I got back to the classroom, everything had changed. I learnt Emily had had an allergic reaction, her mouth and her whole face had swelled up, and she was taken to the hospital. Mia was in the principal's office. When the teachers scolded her, called her evil, she said nothing and looked down, refusing to make eye contact. She looked like she was smiling to herself. It infuriated them further.

But when she saw me afterwards, she was upset and said quietly, 'I didn't mean to. Wasn't gammon with her or anything. You know that, right? I got 'em confused.'

I kicked at a stone in our path. I was angry. She was suspended for a week and I wouldn't get to see her. The principal said he showed some leniency in not expelling her because the next school was an hour away.

I walked her home. We were a street away from her house when we both turned around at the sound of a car zipping behind. It was Mick Hammer and his crew, his

32

brother, Ant, driving. They screamed at Mia as they went past, and screeched the car to a halt in the middle of the road.

The shriek made my chest heave. I started to walk right around the car, though Mia wasn't following.

'I just want to ask if she's okay,' Mia said.

'No,' I said, dragging her. 'C'mon.'

We were almost running when we stepped off the road. I didn't get her going fast enough for her not to hear Mick's spray; he yelled he was going to kill her. We raced each other to her house; I let her win and she knew it.

'When am I going to see you again?' I said, forlorn and not out of breath. I stared up into her honey-brown eyes.

She must have known I wanted to hug her because she folded her arms across her chest. 'We'll meet every day at the hill, okay? At four.'

'You better,' I said.

'No doubt 'bout it.'

It was only when I turned away that I saw her house had been pelted with shit. I drew my eyes away from the sight and to the letterbox on the street – it was crowded with envelopes. I opened them all. Some had already been opened but stuffed back in. It must have been weeks' worth. Hate mail. Mia hadn't told me.

By the next day I had forgotten about Mick and the others, I was dreaming of my life with Mia. The curve of her neck, those legs on show. In the classroom I observed the other girls and wondered why I didn't feel the thump like I did for her.

33

When the bell rang I slapped my backpack on and ran to the hill. I was there until 5 p.m. before I realised she wasn't coming. She must have only been around me because of proximity. Now that she didn't have to anymore she had no interest.

Even Mum's warm shortbread didn't help. My grand-mother said, 'Cheer up, grandson. You are too young to be looking backwards.'

I retired to my bedroom early, surprising both of them.

I heard my grandmother tread labouredly to my door. 'Don't you want to hear a story tonight? Mum has a pie in the oven.'

'No stories,' I said.

The call at 9 p.m. sat me up. Nobody ever called us. No one else in our family paid their phone bill, our rellies just showed up at the house and didn't let us know they were coming.

My mother was whispering and when she saw me her eyes got smaller.

'What is it?'

'Go to bed, Colin. I'm going out. Stay with Nana and I want you to do everything she tells you to do.'

I stood tall. She saw I wasn't going to move.

She said, 'Mia hasn't come home ...'

Our headlights found Mia's shirt, floating like a dollar note in the dust and mist of the night. We stopped the car and her guardian got out first. The way she ran down the bank I knew she had located Mia. I shut the door against my side when I got out, but the sharp and immediate pain paled to the thwack of the horror I got when I saw Mia bent over herself in the grass.

At first it was like I didn't understand why there was so much blood. I thought the leeches had got her. They were bad down there in the swampy area. As my mother moved past me to Mia I registered the mud on her cheeks and underneath her eyes. Her stomach was raw skin and there was blood growing on her jeans.

We raced to the hospital, surged through the Emergency doors and were hit with a buffer. The white women whispering, 'Rape doesn't take priority to heart attack. You're going to have to sit down.'

I snatched the television remote from the woman, pulling it apart like Lego blocks and smashing it under my feet.

Mia was making her first noises of hurt. And the woman kept whispering, 'They're all crazy, twisted, that's right. Out of control.'

I heard that when they asked Mia, 'Who?' she closed her eyes and started to tremble.

It was a few days until I got to see her in the hospital room. Mia wouldn't look up at me, and I was afraid to get too close.

I knew it was the best thing for Mia to move away, but for a long while, all through high school especially, I thought about her dying every night. I couldn't shake it. As soon as I could I left the mountain and the stories behind.

Years later, when I did find myself missing it all, prodding for a former version of me that wasn't sculpted in anger – what do they say in Sydney: Aboriginal men are always angry – it was maybe too late; my grandmother had gone and my mother was an old woman who had turned timid. The Hill End Road house of generations had been sold and the mountain was out of my mind's eye. I wasn't a bush boy anymore, not a bush man. I had been in Sydney for almost a decade. I had stopped ticking the box. I thought, what's the point? By then I had seen Mia at least three times: on the Parramatta train, in the Chinatown food court and dancing in a flash club on Oxford Street. She told me if I was going to make my way back home I'd better do it soon before the dust had covered my tracks.

Skin

Outside, a rosella perched shyly on the edge of the bird bath. Marie watched her daughter, Irma, light up when she saw the bird, and she stumbled towards it. Marie soon noticed there was another rosella there, a smaller one. Irma's hair shone a bronze colour. She and the pair of birds coexisted in the outside space in the shade for the afternoon. Marie looked up after every shirt she folded. There was something about seeing your darling when she didn't know she was being watched. She felt Irma close to her skin. The sun interchanged. Irma's mouth moved against her cheek, speaking words into the passage. Her thumb rested between her lips and nose.

Evidently an afternoon often changed quickly in the valley. The air wolfish, the sky pale lilac, growing dark too soon. Irma lifted her head when her father spread out of the screen door and told her to come inside. Griffin had his arm around her shoulders as they came in together.

'Quite breezy, isn't it?' he remarked, closing both doors behind them.

'I can hear it,' Marie said. She put the washing basket down and bent to touch a piece of Irma's hair, stuck to her cheek.

'You hungry, darling?'

Irma nodded, still mute in her imaginings.

'Dinner will be ready soon.'

Their son, Pete, had found the dog and held it across its belly like a teddy bear. He had spent most of the day in bed with a head cold. Marie picked up honey from the woman, June, who lived around the corner, and spun it into strong tea. Pete didn't like hot drinks and let it cool on the bedside, so when she fetched his empty mug the honey had sunk to the bottom like sand in the ocean.

When the weather turned this way they were reminded of the thin structure they lived in. The plates in the cabinet shook for three minutes. Griffin moved quickly to shut every window in the house, so what resulted was a closed feeling, a whirling sound that haunted a part in Marie's consciousness, an old anxiety, not forgotten.

The gust passed and Marie and Griffin and the children went out the back to look at the foggy calm. When her sister Pearl came wading through the long grass, her hands on the hips of the ironbarks, part of Marie was unsurprised to even call out, 'I knew the wind would bring you.' Griffin and Marie hurried down the slope to help her – she was a dirty weight, belly protruding in her sweaty white dress, mud on her knees.

'My goodness,' Marie said, rubbing Pearl's cheek in an effort to warm her, for as usual her skin was parched.

Pearl said, 'I need to eat.'

'Oh, love, of course,' Marie said. 'I've got a pie in the oven. I'll bring a piece to you.'

They helped her up the stairs and into the house. Griffin set her down in the armchair with a blanket on her knees.

He got a bucket for her to soak her bloodied toes. Marie conjured from the kitchen a thick piece of meat pie, a tall glass of freshly squeezed apple juice and a cup of tea, and put it in front of her.

The children sat silent on the floor, eyes on Pearl. Pearl ignored the children, their names didn't pass her lips; she had forgotten them. Even they saw she was pregnant. Her breasts squirmed out of her dress.

'Not the pie, then?' Marie said. 'A boiled egg?'

Pearl agreed to the egg, hard-boiled, and small cut squares of pan-cooked bread. She ate while Marie got the children ready for bed.

Marie bathed Pearl. Naked, Pearl was excess skin. After the initial surprise of her size, she was beautiful as she always was, a different beauty now. She was full with a fluid whistling under her skin.

Pete's gruff cough came through the wall, a cough that seemed older than him. Marie tested a smile on her sister. 'A boy? Or a girl? I wonder.'

Pearl's face remained blank and Marie let all talk of the baby fold, the where, when, who. She bit her tongue at the need to say how wonderful it was to be a mother and to tell her sister how her life would change. Pearl didn't seem like she wanted to be pressured with this sort of talk. In the morning, Marie would see if Pearl wanted a doctor. There might be a problem finding someone to see her. They'd have to make do. Pearl had come to her for a reason.

After the bath, Marie dried Pearl, starting at her ankles, moving up her legs to her waist. Pearl's shoulders were high and tense. She said there was no need to dry her hair. Marie set her up in Irma's bed. Pearl's webbed feet reached the wall. Pearl spoke bitterly of her backache, and the sleep the baby had taken from her.

'I am going to look after you,' Marie said. She paused, and reached out to rub Pearl's stomach. 'The two of you.'

Pearl bit her nails like she had when she was a child. Her lips were blistered.

'It will all turn out fine.' Marie patted her again.

Griffin was in bed when she got to their room. He gave her a look that she knew he had been saving until they were alone.

'I thought she ...'

'I did, too,' she said.

'Is she going to stay here?'

She nodded.

Griffin nodded in agreement. 'I wonder where she's been all this time.'

'I won't ask her. Not yet. She's been through a lot.'

She turned the light off and got into bed. She was careful not to shift too much next to him to get herself comfortable. It was an old mattress, and you could get stuck into a groove. It went quiet. A few moments later, Griffin added, 'I'm more worried about the children.'

'They will get to know each other. Fine, you will see.' Already Marie was turning towards the side of the bed. 'I'm going to check on her.'

'Marie?' Griffin called her.

'Yes?'

'Come 'ere.'

She put her head against his chest and he brought her hands into his. He let go of her for a second to adjust himself under the sheet. He then moved her hand to slide into his pants.

'Yes,' he said. He sighed deeply.

'Is this the right way for you? The best I can?'

'A bit … yes.'

She repeated her movements for a few minutes.

'Hang on,' he said, springing up. 'I think I need to go. I'll be quick.'

~

Adopted into the Martin family in a house in Bardon, Griffin had never known his birth family. He had skin like pencil, thick eyebrows, and was large handed and awkwardly handsome at seventeen. He had gone to a private boys' school and been chosen to represent his country in the national school cricket championships. At seventeen, boys were men.

He had to travel down to the coast to represent the school for a function. He no longer remembered what it was for, or any detail, just that when he drove away from the function he got hopelessly lost. That night he was alone for the first time, without his team or his parents. His father was a doctor and his mother was a nurse and they had wanted to go with him, but that night they were both working and Griffin had said, insisted, that he didn't need them there.

His father had just bought him a car. A red Datsun. It was hard luck he couldn't find his way back. His new car, he soon realised, had a temperament that wasn't cooperative.

He began to smell something and looked through the window at smoke pummelling from the engine. He stopped the car by the side of the dirt road and got out to inspect the bonnet warily. He didn't know what to do – wait or go find some help. He didn't have the slightest idea of where he was. It was dark. The streets led nowhere.

Griffin walked for a while, looking for a house or someone he could ask. He saw a light in a park. There was an Aboriginal family grouped together, food cooking over a fire, and he was hungry. They saw him standing there. Marie, fifteen, was the one prodding the fish with a stick. The fire was a colour he had only seen in zinc. He walked forward. That image marked his life. Marie, a dust-coloured girl, fed him fish in a park.

When he took the piece of fish from her she glowed with the fire as she smiled. He saw the dark corners of her eyes, and he smiled, too. The fish tasted taut and sinewy, with a layer of sweet oil, the juices dripping down his chin.

Brought back to life by these first few bites, he saw Marie's sister. She lay out in the grass, neck elongated, under an ironbark tree, humming to herself. When she moved to look at him, he turned away.

Marie's cousins and brothers came with him to the car. Nocturnal like all youths, they were wired for the late hours, and rowdy, stirring the empty streets. This was their territory, Griffin understood; they didn't need a sign or paperwork.

'That can't be your car!' they said, rushing to it excit-edly, stroking the smooth red top. They laughed and joked with him as if he was one of them. These muscly dark boys pushed the car down the street to the service station. There was no room left to touch an inch of the car, so he walked beside them, feeling foolish at first. On the way he told them something about himself: he wanted to play cricket for Australia.

'They're not going to pick you,' Marie's brother, the age of an uncle said. 'No black's ever going to get on the team.'

Griffin's dad would have disagreed with him. He told Griffin he would make it. He'd been bowling Griffin out the back since he was a toddler. At the service station, Griffin called his father to pick him up.

When he came back out the fellas shook his hand and said, 'Come over here anytime. You know where we are.'

One of them stood forward for the group and said, 'You like our sister, eh?'

Griffin felt his face turn plum.

'If you hurt a sister of ours, there'll be trouble.' They exchanged wild smiles.

When Griffin got back to Brisbane and told his family of his encounter; they did not like it.

'They are not your sort,' his father said firmly.

In conversation with his parents, Griffin agreed with their interests, looking down into his tea. He told them only what they wanted to hear. But the minute his car was fixed he was down the highway again.

He soon lost count of the times he stood by Marie's door, and she came out, always smiling, looking like the first time he'd seen her. Marie's family made sure there was no chance he was related, and they weren't breaking rules of kinship. It was a two-year courtship, in which time they were never left alone together, even chaperoned to the cinema by Marie's Aunty. They were married in a church in Mudgeeraba.

Griffin's parents had a section of the house for them, and they moved in. On their wedding night, they drove quickly down the coast when they heard the news that one of Marie's brothers had died by electrocution. This brother had told Griffin, just before the wedding, that he was part of the family now.

A short time after they married, Marie heard her father was getting close to returning to the earth. As the eldest daughter, she would be the one to look after him while he died. Griffin would not deny her that. They moved to Hune Hill. Griffin's car wasn't the prized possession it had once been, with scratches and dents on the side. He had stopped playing cricket, and, not long after the conception of their first child, enlisted in the war.

~

Over the next months, as she looked ready, Pearl became increasingly agitated. She lay in the bath, the only place she felt some relief.

'I can't do this anymore,' she said to her sister.

'We can handle it,' Marie said.

Marie took care of her sister, responding to any requests. Her darling Irma was her little helper, assisting her with the meals and the garden while Griffin worked long hours at the butcher shop.

Pearl said sometimes she thought the baby would kill her. She had gotten so ill-proportionally big that she could

44

no longer use the front or back door of the house. She got in and out for an occasional smoke, or for a wander into the bush, through the kitchen window. Marie had given up wondering why this was easier for her. She watched Pearl put her bottom down on the ledge, tilt her hips, and push her feet forward. Perhaps the doorways didn't invite her path. Her body was moving to the ironbarks – called by a mysterious pre-natal rhythm. Marie made sure the windowsill was clear of clutter: kitchen utensils, matches and children's teeth. She kept the window open.

Every day Marie felt distressed that she lacked the knowledge to help her sister. She tried to remember how the old women had helped to deliver her own children. But all of her children had come early, quickly, and much of it was a blur. It was clear this baby of Pearl's was late. When she felt the baby it had turned, ready for delivery. She thought it could be dead until it moved unexpectedly under her fingers. Without acting on the old people knowledge, or white medicine, she was helpless. They had tried everything. Marie had walked with Pearl for hours at a time each afternoon, tracing their tracks through the dry, dull earth, and maintained morning massages and cups of herbal tea.

Leaving Pearl in the bath, Marie and Irma went for a visit to the cemetery. The girl was like her; the toxins in the house weren't doing her good. She hinged on emotion. They walked through the scrub up the hill. They said this place was a lightning point because of the history here. She made out the small white sticks in the ground. The Kresinger circle. Here was where her unborn and stillborn babies also lay, with their ancestors' bones.

There was a bench under an ironbark tree. She sat Irma on her lap, pressed the warm back of her head against her breast. She could see the whole valley from here. She spoke low, the words that she knew rumbling through, the wind making a part. Irma was serious in concentration with her, in connection.

She didn't feel lighter as she usually did talking with the old people. There was no sudden clarity. She saw Irma's fist around something.

'What have you got, my baby?'

Irma opened her hand to a small finger lime. 'Can we go home now?' she whispered.

'Yes, we can,' Marie said.

On the way down from the hill she saw finger limes everywhere. She picked them up and carried them in her skirt. She had seven. Irma skipped ahead of her, the backs of her feet peppered black.

Marie put down the handful of fruit on the kitchen bench. She thumbed her way through an old baking book. Pineapples and other fruit can induce labour, she had read once, and here she read it again. On the next page was a baked key lime tart recipe. Cooking was a calm in chaos – passed on by the women who had shaped her – Marie had learnt to solve problems with method. By the next morning she had organised as best she could a foolproof ensemble of ingredients. The kitchen was her base while Irma and Pete were at school, Griffin was at work and Pearl was resting in the bath. She opened the limes, used the juice and skin, a scatter of macadamia nuts from the tree out the front, cream, avocado and honey. She set the tart in the oven. It had pale and mysterious energy, pulsing there. She watched it with great anticipation. She did not tell Pearl of her exact plans, but hoped her sister would start to smell the tart from where she lay, ridden in the bathwater, and a comforting mystery would take shape.

While the tart was baking, June from down the road came to the door. Pete had a fever, June said. The school had rung, and they wouldn't keep him there. With Griffin at work, Marie knew she had to walk the fifteen-odd minutes to get Pete. The tart was intended to stay in the oven for twenty-five minutes.

Marie ran through the heat, sweat seeping into her eyes. Her feet ached in her poorly worn shoes. She thought about Pete, always getting sick. Griffin said he spent too much time indoors, doing women's work. When she arrived, Pete was standing outside the school office, holding his forehead. She kissed him and held him to her.

'I'm so sorry, my son,' she said. 'We're going to have to rush home.'

When they were children, she and Pearl walked everywhere, barefoot. They followed her father through the country. He showed them the dirt patterns. Pearl, her only whole blood sibling, didn't look like her; she was darker, stronger-looking. They didn't look alike even as children. Pearl had eyes that had been watching for a lot longer than when she was born.

Marie and Pete made it to the house, bringing the heat in. She carried Pete up the stairs and he was asleep before he was in bed. She pulled the blanket halfway up his sweating, small body.

She opened the oven and there the finger lime tart was, just ready, edges brown but not burnt. Her hand tingled from the heat as she pulled it out, but no worry – this speciality was for her sister and she had prepared it.

She walked up to the bathroom, pushing open the door. The curtains had been pulled half over the window. The first thing she saw was Pearl's stomach, floating above the water's surface. Pearl's eyes were shut. There was an arm of a different skin tone around her chest, below her large, floating breasts. Two people were in the bathtub. The two people, her sister and her husband, were in a terrible tangle or a struggle or some kind. Griffin was behind Pearl, half of his face showing behind her hair, his shoulders against the wall. He was moving, and the colourless water was running around them as if it couldn't keep up. They opened up their eyes and saw her, but their bodies stayed where they were.

Marie went downstairs and pulled out the knife to cut a slice of the pie, which was cooling on a rack next to the oven. She delicately transferred the piece onto a gold-rimmed plate and added a coin-sized dollop of fresh cream beside it. She waited. Griffin appeared, and said he was going back to work, his hair half-wet. The car roared out onto the street.

In a few minutes, Pearl came down the stairs in her white dress. Marie put the plate in front of her. Pearl sat on the same chair she had sat on when she first came to the house, the chair that had become hers during her stay, a chair that had originally belonged to their mother. The room was full of family items. In a bowl next to Pearl were their father's clapsticks, which he had made himself using unblemished, light wood. Pearl used her hands to bring the pie to her mouth, nodding in approval at the taste. There were no crumbs left when she handed Marie back the plate.

After she finished, Pearl slid herself out the window to go for an afternoon smoke. Marie took the plate to the sink and put the rest of the pie in the fridge, with the knife resting on top. She reached over the bench to shut the kitchen window. The heat was immediately trapped. She got a handful of face washers out of the linen cupboard and ran them under the tap. Irma, who had been playing in the yard, came inside, her face flushed. She presented in front of her mother, opening her palms to a lady beetle, which flew up, grazing the girl's nose. The beetle went towards the closed window. Marie stuck a washer on Irma's neck. They heard a tapping, a prodding.

'Don't open the window, dear,' she said.

Irma nodded. They both looked outside at the same time. Pearl was staring straight at them with a sickening glare. One hand on her back and one on her stomach, she was huge and hurting. Her dress flipped up in the wind and her stomach demanded viewing. Marie quickly moved away from the kitchen. She walked upstairs to Pete's room. He was sleeping, his hands under his cheek. She got in beside him and pushed the cold washer on to the dent of his back. It was like throwing an ice cube into a fire. She hugged him to her, the clammy warmth of his arms and the drowsy muffle of the bed. She wasn't sure if she was sleeping.

She was rattled by Irma's voice at the door. 'Mum, you gotta come. Aunty is havin' a baby out the front.'

★

49

Pearl was in the currents of contractions outside the house. She was kneeling directly in line with the front door, facing the street. Marie and Irma got her down on the ground, one hand on either of her shoulders. Her breath was citrus and smoke. The water on the ground sizzled from the sun. Pearl's eyes widened and Marie held on to her. No cars went by and no one saw them, but at the same time the valley saw them. The open sky fingering their skin.

This was where the sisters had been born, in the shadows of the ironbarks, the spot where their women had given birth for a continuum of years. Pearl made little sound as she pushed. She didn't cry out. Sweat broke across her back. She leant forward, her head on her arms, her legs swaying from side to side, her toes clenched together. Above, the leaves stirred with wind. She moved back to her hands and knees, head up. A fierce whisper escaped her lips but no words were understood.

For Marie, it was quick and there was nothing to be done. A few minutes and a few tries and it was Irma that had her hands where they needed to be. She took the baby from Irma's arms, the wet blood shared across their arms. He made a sound that imprinted on her.

A while later, they sat in the kitchen on the chairs, eating the remaining pie out of the dish. Pearl was newly energised and talkative. Irma was proud. Marie tried to feel relief. The baby was solid and soft. She had weighed him on the kitchen scales, 4.6 kilograms. She sat with the baby wrapped in a white blanket, his eyes opened when she looked at him. He had a thick grey casing of hair on his head.

Pearl moved through the kitchen and opened the window near the sink, looking out into the bush. Her hair moved a bit as she turned.

She spoke. 'You said you would look after him.'

Marie slowly shook her head. 'He is your child.'

'You can understand why I can't take it with me. It would be good here. A brother for Irma and Peter. A gift. A birthday present.'

Marie shut her eyes for a moment.

'Of course,' her sister said, smiling. 'I wouldn't forget your birthday.' She leant forward and gave her a kiss on her cheek.

Marie looked down at the baby in her arms. She didn't move as Pearl bent her knees and pushed her body through the sun-lined window. She could hear her sister's feet touch the ground and her firm, wet steps as she went back the way she came.

'A decent size, this little bloke,' Griffin said when he got home. 'Well done.'

They named the baby Charles, after Griffin's father, and Jack, after her father. He was Charles Jack Kresinger, for all her children kept their grandfather's name. He wasn't painted up proper way, and there was no ceremony, the clapsticks had disappeared from the house, but Marie knew he'd grow up Kresinger; she knew how to do it right.

Crash

Two cars raced up the mountain in the night. A white Subaru and a grey four wheel-drive. There was just the one road, a steep, winding one, with none of the safety rails or signs you see implemented now.

The first car, the white one, was driven by Lena. Lena, Mrs Kresinger, was thinking of the last thing her husband said to her. He'd come home with the eggs she needed for the pastry, none of them broken, he'd put a hand on her waist and said, 'Lena, I'm going to take you for a drive soon. Just the two of us.'

She had smiled in surprise, that small moment spurring something. She had loved him for ten years and he still did that to her.

Janet Jensen had loved him for the same amount of time. She'd never admit to him she noticed him first. Dark seductive eyelashes, long hair, and that body. She watched him from her office on George Street; bare-chested, he led protests against anti-march laws, holding signs and swearing through a microphone. At night, when she finished late she saw him, now with a shirt on, stumbling out of bars, always followed by a blonde white girl, both off their faces. She'd seen him swagger around the city and thought, that's the kind of man I want, but I know that's all wrong.

She worked as a junior clerk at the law firm. She'd been highly ambitious from a young age, and raised in a well-off family, which gave her the opportunity to study with some of the groundbreakers of the time at the University of Queensland, and it wasn't too long before she was a qualified lawyer.

Charlie and two of his mates, Doug Hall and Ronnie Blake, were fighting charges of assault on police in a demonstration. She noticed the surprise in his face when she was introduced as their lawyer. His first words to her were a challenge: 'What does a pretty rich white girl like you know about politics?'

But she ended up being his match. Quiet, with a biting intelligence, she spoke slowly and with grace. He learnt to listen. She was never going to say anything that would land her in trouble, but he got her talking dirty.

She was behind the wheel of the second car, the four wheel-drive. Her husband, Gary, said women were ill-suited to drive a car like that. Janet had found some recklessness in her forties.

Both women had heard Charlie Kresinger's bike had tumbled off the top. Not long after a passer-by had called Emergency, the news had travelled through the town. Call it Goorie grapevine or women's intuition, but they both knew fast.

Janet Jensen hadn't been in town long. Her husband had bought a holiday home, on the bay, with a view of the ocean. They'd had the place for over a year but this was the first time Gary could get away. The kids were on school holidays. Janet was catching up on her reading, and catching up on Charlie, finding out all about him through the chatty locals.

Janet hadn't seen Charlie for years, but just the day before, they'd run into each other in the organics store. He had cut off his dreads. He still looked thirty, fit – the bronzed young warrior she remembered. While they stood together in the aisle, she recalled how she would always push his dreads to the side, an unconscious habit when they were talking. She put her hand up, but now she had to touch his cheek. Firm, large. A man's cheek.

He didn't flinch. He looked at her with his dark eyes; he reminded her of an American Indian. When she looked at him she remembered him, remembered his dreads flicking in her face as they kissed on the waterfront, a decade ago. The dreads had a stretch of pure silver in them, like the edge of a wave. He kept them in a ponytail only when he surfed or rode, and wore them loose when he walked around town, relaxed and salt-silly from a duck-in, seawater on his lips.

Charlie touched his face where Janet had touched him. She noticed a dark mole on the opposite cheek that she was sure had never been there before. She was fascinated by his difference.

'Married?' he asked her.

'Yes,' she answered. 'Gary's a chef.'

'Gary or Gravy?' he answered, but dully, without a smile, as if the effort to joke was too predictable and no longer fun.

They reached the cash register.

'After you,' he said, with an elaborate gesture.

She paid for her groceries. He put the bananas and peanut paste down, and reached for his wallet. She had to speak.

'Can we——'

'Go for coffee sometime?' He winked. 'Sure.'

Coffee would lead to something, she knew. Open up the precious space between them once more. Now, as she drove, she thought repeatedly – please let it not be the last time I see him, the last thing I say to him.

He had driven up the mountain, maybe drunk – irresponsible, even for Charlie. With that, you couldn't help but start to think about things. Was he suicidal? Janet wondered. What could cause him to be suicidal? Seeing her yesterday? That he loved her but couldn't be with her?

When Janet turned the bend she saw the white car ahead. They were both speeding. Janet wanted to overtake, but the other car gave her no room, not that there was much on this stretch of road. Then she recognised the driver. They both recognised each other, Janet by the other woman's long luscious hair in plaits, Lena via the rear-view mirror, the nose. With a groan, Janet put her foot on the pedal and sped up; she went off the road and up the terrain, following a dirt trail used as maintenance.

Lena shook her head at the sight of the other vehicle climbing, disappearing up the bare incline. She kept a steady speed, going carefully around the corners. What use would she be to Charlie not alive? She needed to reach him in one piece.

Charlie had taught Lena to drive when their daughter was four. She was a natural, he said. A much better driver than he was. There is something about women who learn to drive after they've become mothers. If she had learnt before, she would be as wild and passionate as she was with anything else. But she was subdued on the road; she took care of herself and others.

She would never tell Charlie to give up the motorcycle. It was him as much as his surfboard and his shark-tooth necklace and earring. Not a fake, he had caught the bastard himself, he said. Different from his brother and sister, and despite being a freshwater man by blood, Charlie felt the lure of the ocean. He used to tear down the coast on his bike at any opportunity, ride back and forth from the city – he had cultural political obligations there – looked up to as a young leader of his mob. But during his expulsion, he decided to live by the beach permanently in a sharehouse in Byron Bay. He loved Byron and the southern beaches. It became a second home to him. He fit in with the surfing and the hippie and artistic scene, the raw food movement. Back then he had dreads that went halfway down his back.

At that time Lena lived in the same sharehouse, mostly rented by uni dropouts who weren't there long enough to leave an imprint. After finding each other, Charlie and Lena stayed there well past the usual time. There were nine of them living in the cramped house; he slept on the balcony in a hammock, she in the second room off the hallway. They'd been living under the same roof for a few weeks, but he was rarely home, and they hadn't had a proper conversation.

It had been two months since she'd left her home in Crete. She'd been backpacking around Australia and was staying in Byron for a while. She danced at the night markets by the beach to make some money. One afternoon he was buttering a slice of toast and she was making coffee at the same time and they both offered each other some. He took an interest, asked what she did. She asked him to come along that night, and that's when he first really saw her.

When he arrived, his eyes were embraced by a wall of colour – orange, yellow, blue and the sexual beat of a drum. He felt an unexplained nervousness for the first time in his life. She was bellydancing in mango scent, candle hue and mosquitoes. As fast as she was moving, he was transfixed by the sweat rolling down her stomach. Lena liked the hot climate, like him, and after they made love, they would sleep in the hammock on the deck, wake up with mosquito bites.

They still made love like teenagers, with the audacity to try something new.

Sweat was forming on the top of Janet's lip. The car was rolling forward of its own accord, she wasn't in control. She could almost see the peak of the mountain.

They'd met again in Brisbane, in a professional context, though at a vulnerable time in each of their lives. Charlie and Lena's child had just started school. Janet had never gotten over him, and it must have been obvious in the way she looked at him in their meetings at a West End cafe.

They worked late, found ways to linger. They grew closer than they had before without being physical. One night he showed up at her door, rain trickling in behind him and she knew, as he knew, what could happen. She didn't want it to be this way.

She reasoned with him. 'You have a beautiful wife, a beautiful child. What are you doing here?'

Trying to get closer, he said, 'Things won't feel resolved for me unless you kiss me. Kiss me and that will be enough.' But as soon as he said it, they both know that it was not true. That the kiss would only open up the mass of feelings and turn those feelings into actions.

'I can't,' she said.

His eyes locked into hers, he showed her his desperation. He took a step up, his chest forward, a hand in his dreads, keeping them from his face. The rain had soaked his sleeves. The necklace moved against his neck, closer to her. And then her words must have sunken in, he remembered himself – let his hair go, and she saw the back of him as quickly as he had come at her. He strode away with a flat stride, detached from the pace of the increasing rain. The swagger had gone.

She wondered what would have happened if she had let him in, if they had started the affair. Just one touch, his hand in hers, a thumb to her lips and she would have lost her objections. She didn't want to be the other woman, but she was never anything else.

She knew the woman Charlie had married was an exotic dancer with browned skin, flowing hair. Why would Charlie bother with a plain Jane like her, when he could go to the Greek islands every day of the week? Lena enjoyed life. From Charlie she knew Lena found vitality in music, was creative, pursued things to abandon, could be like a child. Janet could never do that. She was too serious, too aware, especially of herself.

Still, she remembered the intelligent conversations about art, politics and philosophy they'd had in the brief times they were together.

'Whatcha reading?' he would say as he came up to her in the cafe, planting a kiss on her cheek, close to the lips.

He was shaped by his parents. He said about his father: 'He was from a rich family. But they gave him away when he married his own kind. They raised him white and the moment he remembered he was black, the moment he tried being himself they left him.' About his mother: 'The strongest woman I've ever met. She would do anything for us.'

Charlie was the youngest, and both women would agree about one thing – he had been spoilt rotten by his mother and his sister, Irma. Janet teased he hadn't learnt to wash himself, except in the sea.

When he talked about being a spokesperson for his mob he often said, 'My ancestors died for me to have this right.'

Janet felt a warmth spread across her hands just from listening to him talk. He was so passionate about his family history, and he had great, wild ideas. He'd look at her like they were going to change the world together.

Gary, on the other hand, was kind, but not wanting. He was, like her, driven by his job, suppressing the need for anything else, things they'd felt when they were younger but no longer believed in.

As Janet drove onward, the road treacherously steep, she had no knowledge of what was ahead of her. She felt a tightness in her chest; she must get to him, clamp her lips down on his. If he died she would be alone.

She pushed down the accelerator and, coming unexpectedly upon the road again, the vehicle lifted off the ground, airborne for a moment, before pummelling back towards the ground and landing on the white car. The back tyres of the four wheel-drive smacked onto the bonnet. The piled cars wobbled. The white car swerved and braked underneath.

Inside, Lena, swearing and screaming in Greek, felt glass fly in her face. Instead of bringing the car to a complete stop then, somehow she accelerated and rushed them forward, closer to the edge, so the other vehicle was rammed at the clifftop. Lena saw the four wheel-drive tilt forward. Down below she saw the lights of the town, and the lit-up bay. Perfect, dark. Lena watched it happen from the outside. She found herself in another scene, back then. Watching on while Charlie loved Janet. The first time she saw Janet she was on the television. Charlie had known to switch it on. There she was, immediate in her beauty and intelligence. When Lena had seen her after that she was always impeccably dressed, a fancy, sophisticated woman who used big words in normal conversation. She couldn't compete with that. And now this woman, not just content with fucking her husband, was here, claiming him again.

Lena felt the gravity in her own car. 'Oh, shit,' she said. She reversed, and the tyres circled the dirt, the engine heaved, then she felt the car roll slowly backwards.

When the car was clear off the cliff's line, Lena tumbled out, falling into the overgrowth. As soon as she got to her feet, she started running. It was only a moment before she heard Janet reach the ground and chase her down the road. Janet reached the shorter woman, grabbed her hands, pulled her around and swung at her. She missed Lena's face and cried out. She put her hands down. They were bleeding.

Lena left her, and continued jogging further up the mountain road. She called her husband's name into the trees. She picked out a shard of glass from her neck.

The red and blue sirens flashed up ahead. There was an exclusion zone around a pair of trees. A motorbike was wedged between them.

The paramedics, standing in a pool of light on the road, stared at the two women approaching. One of the paramedics on duty that night, a Murri one, would say he had never been more frightened at the sight of them appearing like spirits.

'My husband,' Lena tried to say, but her voice got caught in her throat when she saw the stretcher.

'My love!' Janet's voice overpowered Lena's.

Charlie lay on the stretcher with a neck brace. A paramedic talked to both women. 'Your husband – he is fine. We're just taking precautions.'

When Lena reached his side, grabbing his fingers and squeezing them, he gripped them back. A smile formed on his half-parted lips. There wasn't a mark or scratch on him.

His voice was thick with a chuckle. 'I'm fine, honey. Just a bump to the head.'

Lena checked twice, pulling his hair to the side. His forehead was clean.

Charlie saw Janet in the distance. He called her closer. His eyes fluttered closed. She was a depth in his ocean, swallowing him. She had three boys, and he always had the feeling one of them was his, but as to which one, he changed his mind each time he saw them.

Also, his wife, still holding his hand. He remembered his delight at the first glance of his daughter's head wrapped up in a green blanket. He knew that Amy had mended any gaps in their marriage that had emerged over the years. She was seven years old now, and most days they managed to exchange a smile, a humorous, tender or wry one, over her. In the days he wasn't there, the times when there were things to do, family business and drives down to the Tent Embassy in Canberra, Lena held things together.

The paramedics pulled the women aside, the concern shifting. Both women were covered in dirt and blood. Lena had glass deep in her chin and pine needles in her hair. Janet's clothes were torn. The paramedics talked to them and checked them out, gathered they both might have whiplash. Two additional neck braces were taken out of the ambulance.

They all piled into the Ambulance together. They stared at the two damaged vehicles as they passed by.

Confined, Lena and Janet faced one another, rocking, both with their backs to a wall, Charlie between them. In that moment, even though they didn't yet know it, the women aligned themselves to a movement separate from Charlie. In the morning, a pick-up truck was sent to collect the motorcycle and the two vehicles. Insurance claims were settled.

The two women met again, a few years later, at the university – Janet's alma mater – in a research trial for whiplash patients. They started talking, and meeting after each session. Lena didn't tell Charlie. By the completion of the trial, they'd become unlikely friends, and revved each other up – they didn't want to waste their lives on a man who was conflicted.

Charlie hadn't made a decision between them in his heart, and he wasn't about to. Lena said it was because he was a Libran. Janet called him a mummy's boy. They continued to meet in secret, calling it book club, sometimes bringing the children along with them to sit in the corner of the cafe. Janet coaxed Lena to ask for a divorce. The twin twinge in their necks – Lena left, Janet right – would remind them in weak moments of the choices to be made.

The two women developed a fondness and respect for each other. Janet was also thinking of getting out of her loveless marriage. She had pushed herself back into work, and had taken up kickboxing, to great effect on her core. Lena had got a better job at a cafe, found a rental property around the corner from it, and had reunited with relatives that had immigrated. Her daughter became playmates with Janet's boys.

When Charlie found out that his wife and Janet were friends, it was a terrifying predicament for him at first. By that time he was living on his own in a house in Brisbane.

The dishes piled up in the sink and the counter was stacked with newspapers he no longer had the energy to read. He had Amy over on the weekends, and she was often quiet. His prized motorbike had been substituted with a lemon, a real poxy thing, handed down from his brother. He reckoned it embarrassed Amy. One afternoon, Amy's teacher called him up at work. Amy had waited for her mother to pick her up from school but she hadn't turned up. Charlie got Amy – she was waiting outside the school office – and they drove to Lena's house, along the main road. There was an area blocked off, but he didn't pay too much attention to it, turning into the street. He used the key under the mat to open the door to the stuffy house he hadn't been in before. He scanned the table for a note, picked up the phone and listened to the messages. It all started to come together as he drove to the hospital. Lena had been hit by two cars while walking across the road to pick up Amy.

At the hospital he rang Janet. She was there, in the room, when they shut down the machine. Janet cried beside the bed. Charlie held Amy, her head under his chin.

He took Amy back to his house. Every night that month they drove the suburbs looking at the Christmas lights. Even if the weather was vicious and the water would leak in by their feet, he wouldn't head home until she fell asleep against the window. He'd carry her up the stairs and she wouldn't stir. The drives seemed to help her sleep better, chase the bad dreams away. On stormy nights they both dreamt intensely, violently – they often drowned. Charlie realised it had always been like this, even before Lena had passed. It so happened that particular summer delivered a record number of storms in the south-east, more than any other year. He gazed at his daughter twitching in her sleep as the wind yowled outside.

WATER

No one checks my ticket as I hop on board the ferry. I am the only one who elects to sit outside, and I soon find out why. The wind. I can already feel my face is beaten, my skin stung, my lips chapped. But I have made myself comfortable, my legs drawn up underneath me, and I am away from the other people so I just sit back and feel the wind in my ears. I must fall asleep because the next thing I notice is a man with a moustache standing over me expectantly.

I look at him for a moment before realising he is the ticket collector. I bend down and rummage through my duffel bag. He stands close to me until I find my ticket and he looks at it carefully before stamping it and giving it back to me.

When I look at it again I realise the lady has given me a return ticket, and I haven't twigged. I won't be needing it – it is only of use today. I am still sleepy, and when I get up my legs are shot with lead so I stumble and drop the ticket overboard. I look over the edge, though the little bit of paper has already been swallowed up by the whitewater surge of the boat, and I feel a misplaced sense of grief.

When I'd told my mother I was going to work on Russell Island, I admitted it was by no means an easy thing, yet I didn't feel any reluctance leaving the mainland and heading off in the ferry, powering through the thrilling surge of ocean. On the way to Russell, we passed the smaller islands; they glinted in the sun.

It isn't long until I guess the shape before us is Russell, and I make out the buildings, the smoke from the industry tankers. There is a lot of greenery, and a thin edge of sand, like icing on a cake. The attendant announces our destination and the ferry stops.

I arrive on a Saturday, so I have a day and a half to settle in before starting on Monday. The contracting company provides a stand-up house at the base on Russell Island. It suits me fine. I thought Russell would be what you expect of an island – peaceful, isolated, good for my thoughts, but it's not. It's a centre of activity, the company is a good way along to completing the 'Australia2' project for the government by the 2028 deadline.

My place is an easy five-minute walk from the ferry, in the quieter residential section. There is a grocery store just by the ferry terminal, convenient, and not too expensive as you would think. My street is full of houses that look exactly like mine. To use my mobile phone, I have to keep walking to the end of the street, and there the industry stand-ups start.

My place is fully furnished. All I have to unpack is my blanket and clothes and a toaster. Everything in the house smells brand new, the off-gassing piping through my lungs.

It is like a hotel room – the bed has sheets on it and the fridge is compact. I'll have to stop myself from leaving the towels on the floor; there won't be anyone around while I'm out.

On the mainland the other week my cousin Julie and I met at the old post office and had a drink. I'm still getting to know Julie. She is twenty years older than me, but she lets me forget it. Julie lives in the apartments in the Story Bridge, built just a few years ago. Julie has lived most of her life in slimehole Sydney, she's only just moved back here. I'm glad Julie called me when she came back and we've been meeting, because I want to get closer to that side of the family. Dad died when I was young. My mum is white and she tells me a bit about my family but I don't know much. I know they were all artists – my dad, Julie's dad, my other uncle and my grandmother. It's not like it used to be for artists. I can't paint; I was lucky, I guess.

Julie also doesn't paint. She works now at the Freedom of Speech office, in the IT department. On her weekends for some extra cash Julie does tarot card readings in her apartment.

We talk about How Things Are Really Shit Now. Julie said it began ten years ago: she was there. In August 2012, a young Tanya Sparkle went to see Hugh Ngo speak at the Gallery of Modern Art. Julie saw Tanya sitting across from her. She could tell, even with the distance between them, that Tanya was slipping out of her skin to ask a question, and sure enough when the audience was called Tanya announced herself, a long, wielded introduction. She gave a spiel about reconciliation, which she stylised to 'recon' and

71

then she said to Hugh, 'I am an optimist. I believe one day Aboriginal people will get back what they lost and more.'

The crowd grew quiet and looked at each other. Julie snickered.

Hugh raised an eyebrow. 'What?' he said. 'Are you mob gonna give us two countries?'

Tanya Sparkle has really thrived as a female leader of this country. Where J. Gill had been a scapegoat, a cardboard target, as hated and painted as strict headmistresses are, it all went right for Tanya.

When Tanya Sparkle became President I was in the pool sticking laps. I got out, dried my legs, and wondered for the first time where everyone was. The women were all on the street.

President Sparkle has made a few significant reforms in her tenure, particularly to Indigenous affairs. Advancement of native title, health, employment, education, creative control and recognition of culture were the main objectives of the policy.

As Julie says, President Sparkle really *shit on* the public transport system. Catching a bus has become a nightmare. Sometimes you'd rather spend your money on a cab. A few years ago, all the route numbers were replaced with language names for destinations, such as Turrbal, causing mass commuter confusion. To start with, there were many inaccuracies in the places and the names, the communities were not consulted. The names they did match up with locations weren't spelt phonetically and not with the community in mind.

It's hard to know what to do at the major bus inter-change. The buses whoosh by and I feel a strong sense of displacement. I'm not sure if it comes from being an Aboriginal person, or if it's as disconcerting for the rest of the public transport users. When it began, I once got on the Turrbal bus thinking I was going to Toombul shopping centre.

Julie tells stories from working at the Freedom of Speech office. I have a friend who actually went to jail over a text message – they search your phone at random any number of times a year for any sort of provocative material, particularly what they call racial violation. It has been three years since the social media ban.

Julie showed me the Census stats recently: Aboriginal spirituality is on its way to becoming the most popular religion. In the churches now it's only white guys preaching.

Just after we became a republic, the Australian anthem was changed to the 2012 Jess Mauboy hit, 'Gotcha'. The national flag is a horrible mash-up job of the old flag and both the Aboriginal flag and the Torres Strait Islander flag. It looks like Tanya Sparkle's seven-year-old son did it in Paint.

Aboriginal art has almost wiped out all other Australian art. A journo said recently in *The Australian*, 'If you're not black, forget it.' The sad thing is, most Aboriginal artists crack under the enormous pressure and celebrity, from the commodification of their work. You only have to look at my family for examples of that.

President Sparkle is determined to leave her legacy on native title. A second 'country' is being built, by using the islands off southern Moreton Bay. If Julie's story is true, Sparkle really did get the idea off Hugh Ngo at that gallery opening. The re-forming company are going to create new land between the twenty or so islands off the Brisbane coastline, joining them to create a super island. This is where Aboriginal people can apply to live. In the application criteria they are required to show how they have been removed or disconnected from their country – priority given to those who don't even know where they've come from. Queensland's the first state to implement the policy, with other states to follow. The community will be effectively self-governed, like the Torres Strait.

What I don't think our President has covered on her list is loss of culture. Young people are growing up and not having a clue who they are or who they should be.

Julie laughs at me, because I've just got this job in the re-forming industry. Yes, I know, I told Julie, they're half our problems, and she can't understand it – but it's much better money than I was getting shooting pigeons for the local council. When the position for a 'Cultural Liaison Officer' came up I thought great, I'd love the chance to work with other Aboriginal people, because that's another way of finding out about my culture and what I missed out on growing up.

Well, the real reason Julie laughed at me when I got back to her after the interview was because I wasn't actually going to be working with Aboriginal people in my Cultural Liaison Officer role.

I'll be working with what they call the 'sandplants'. There's a lot of talk about them in the media lately, all sensationalist crap, I reckon, like asylum seekers in the naughties. I don't really know much about them to be honest. I don't want to call them 'sandplants' – 'sandpeople' or 'plantpeople' seems more sensitive, but I don't know which to use.

On Monday, I head on foot to the Science Centre on the other side of the island. From my house, facing out, I'd seen three brightly coloured temporary buildings, oddly shaped. The Science Centre is the red temporary building. This is where I find our office, around the side, and meet my boss, Milligan. He seems alright, easy to talk to. He doesn't look like what I pictured; he doesn't have a beard or glasses.

Milligan had explained already on the phone that it was really a 'hands-on' sort of job. I wasn't going to be sitting down behind a desk sipping from an eco-cup nine-to-five like Julie did. I had to get out and talk to these plantpeople, and this required taking the company's tinny out to the smaller desolate islands on the rough edges of Russell. Milligan had told me this so I could show up with the proper gear: jeans, boots, company polo and a bag they'd given me, horribly flimsy, like one you'd get from a conference.

Milligan assures me that steering the boat is really easy, though I am glad to hear it when he says he's taking me out the first time.

Two or so weeks earlier, when I'd found out I got the job, Milligan sent me by email quite a bit of material to study beforehand. It included research papers on the plantpeople, newspaper clippings and official guvvie policy papers. I have to admit I only really started reading through it last night, but I feel I know a lot more about them now.

These creatures, beings, I'm not yet comfortable on how to place them, were formed when they started experimenting here, mining the sea in preparation for the islandising. It was a young botanist (I know this, as he is a friend of Milligan's) who first discovered them: he distinguished their green human-like heads lined up on the banks of Russell Island. A lot doesn't make much sense to me yet. I have a feeling the documents don't say everything.

Right from the start, the government has been very protective of them, so they don't become a public spectacle. You need permission from a government official to go near the population.

Basically, they present a problem for the Project at this stage, as all the southern Moreton Bay islands are being evacuated. This means everyone has to leave their homes and businesses for an indeterminate amount of time while the engineers work on the re-forming. These plantpeople, who divide their time between the water, Russell Island and the edges of some of the smaller unoccupied islands, must cooperate during the process, for the safety of all.

Some of them 'root' – that is, they firm their roots to an area, into the ground, and are hard to persuade to move; you can't get them away. Milligan tells me there are a few that actively voice their opinions within the community, speaking out against the government and their plans.

They are a very intelligent species. I read a transcript of an interview with one of them. She spoke well, from the notes, a steady, formalistic English. Hers was the only first-person account and insight I have into what these people are about. A plant's mind.

The government doesn't know the exact number of the population, anywhere from seventy to a hundred is their guess. The plantpeople mostly used to inhabit Russell Island, but since the government has moved in, they have split to the closest islands.

Some of the plantpeople are regularly called in to the Science Centre for testing. They call them 'specimens' here, I notice, and I try to follow suit but it's an odd word on my tongue.

During my induction I sit down with my boss in his office and we have a meeting with Sophie, the admin girl, also present. My boss tells me to 'keep things as peaceful as possible'. He suggests I talk to the leader. Her name is Larapinta. Sophie adds, 'there is Hinter, too.' Milligan says, 'but he's more difficult.'

Milligan tells me Sophie will take me on a tour of the facility and sort out my paperwork. He says he'll take me out on the tinny on Thursday, and I assume it's the last I'll see of him today. I hope Sophie will sort everything out quickly; the waiting around part of a new job always stresses me out. I just want to get started and learn the ropes as soon as I can. Sophie takes me out of the office section and shows me the laboratories, loading dock and the examination rooms. After a while, I don't really bother remembering people's names.

She swipes us back into our office space and puts me at a currently unoccupied desk. She downloads the paperwork for a security pass and gets me to fill it in. In between filling in other forms, I go to the water cooler and I grab a plastic cup from up the top.

Then I see Milligan coming back. 'Larapinta's here now,' he says. 'Meeting room one.'

'Oh, right,' I say, and straighten up. I hear my boots tap against the temporary, cheap wooden tiles as I walk down the hall. I don't know where to go and walk around for a while from door to door, but I eventually remember the meeting rooms are just after the toilets, next to the examination room.

There are two sandplants standing outside the exam room. I walk past quickly. Seeing them for the first time, I am struck both by how startlingly human-like they are, and how alarmingly unhuman they are. Green, like something you would see in a comic strip, but they are real.

I walk into the meeting room and Larapinta is there, sitting at the table.

Larapinta is less green than the others. She has wild frond-like hair across her face, bleached pale pink in parts, perhaps from the sun. She has a face that's like me and you. With space for two small eyes and a hint of a mouth. Am I blind not to notice much difference? Of course there is the body of them, shaped like a post, covered in prickles except for the hands. Both the females and the males are identical. She has no breasts. I understand they are ungendered; see, their gender is not predetermined and is only communicated.

'I'm sorry about how they've been treating you,' I say immediately. 'I want to tell you I'm here to mediate. I will listen to your needs and try to make it work. That's my job.'

'Thank you,' she says. 'Water?'

I realise I am still holding the styrofoam cup, which is empty.

She tops up my cup with her hand. She holds three of her fingers together and a small flow of clear water squeezes out and into the cup.

'You're a native Australian?' she asks.

I'm taken aback by her observation. I'm not yet used to her forthright nature. 'Yes.'

'Where is your ancestral home?'

'The islands here, actually,' I say.

She nods unemotionally. 'Which island?'

I frown. 'Ki Island, I think. I've never been there. My father died, see.'

'I see,' she says. 'How did he die? He must have been extraordinarily young. Human men live to eighty-two.'

'He killed himself.'

Larapinta blinks to register. 'Doesn't this upset you?'

'My dad? Of course ...'

'The mining. The islandising. Australia2.' She's blunt.

'Oh, I don't know. Like I said, I've never been there. How can you have an attachment to a place you've never been?'

She walks off to the far side of the room and takes something in her hands.

I talk to her back. 'I thought you weren't political.'

'There isn't anything that isn't political.' It's an expression that sounds human, but everything in her voice indicates she is not.

I look closer at what she is doing. It is an e-reader she is holding.

'I have been reading,' she says. 'I come here to charge it up and use the wi-fi to download more material.'

I nod, and take a sip from the cup.

Wednesday is a public holiday. On Tuesday night, after a day getting a grip, I catch the ferry back to the mainland in a dark so stiff my hands are part of it. It is cold, too, with the wind.

While I'm on the ferry I look occasionally to the left and wonder where in the darkness Ki Island is. My father and his brothers were raised by my grandmother on Ki. I wonder if the island is anything like Russell, or the smaller, overgrown, brown isles I've passed. Remembering the stories my father told me about growing up is like walking on glass stairs in my mind.

I transfer to the bus that says 'Kurilpa', and it stops me into the city. When I walk in, Julie is already at the bar. She has let her hair out natural, and she looks different, like I haven't seen her for a while, or I've just really seen her from far away, and I've realised we are strangers to each other still.

'Kaden!' she says. 'Were you okay getting into town? I sometimes forget it gets dark so quickly up here. I miss daylight saving.'

I chuckle a little. 'I'm fine. It's a piece of cake compared to what driving a box over water is going to be like!'

She widens her eyes, nods, 'How were your first two days on the job?'

I tell her a quick story about Milligan and how he seems uncomfortable around the plantpeople that come into the centre. 'But how is Uncle Ron?' I ask.

'Dad's ... good. He's been sick, again, though.'

I nod. 'I would like to visit him on Ki.'

'Can't,' Julie says. 'Evacuated, remember?'

Already. I didn't think they were moving so fast. I put my hand to my forehead. 'Where is Uncle now?'

Julie shrugs. 'Around, really. Sometimes in the home in Gympie. With me. At the hospital.'

I nod.

'You'll see him soon, I hope. This is not one of his best weeks, but I'll tell him you're going to stop by. He'd love that.'

We talk about Julie's work and then, when we've exhausted the topic, I take a big sip from my glass and ask, 'Do you remember much about me and my dad when I was little?'

Julie thinks about it for a moment. 'When you were really young, five or something, I used to babysit you all the time. I was studying and staying on campus, and my uni was just around the corner from where you used to live. And the family was always getting together, back then, your dad and my dad were so very close, even with the age distance.'

'Then Dad died.'

'Yeah, and I guess it pulled the family apart. We all tried to help you and your mum. I'm not sure about some of it because the next year I moved to Sydney. And Dad and Uncle Theo were always so heavily involved politically. I think they really threw themselves in it after your dad died.'

I tell Julie, 'I felt really alone growing up, like I didn't know my family.'

'I'm sorry, Kaden.' Julie sighs. 'Do you remember when you came down to visit me that weekend? You were sixteen and you had just come out to your mum and she didn't take it too well so you came and saw me in Sydney. I snuck you in to the burlesque show and you got sick after sharing one bottle with me.'

I smile with a mixture of humiliation and recognition. 'You remember that?'

'Of course I do! It was a good weekend, in the end. And I was glad you came to me, even though your mother didn't like me too much for it at the time.'

I nod. 'It was Pancakes on the Rocks.'

'Hey?'

'It was all the chocolate pancakes that made me sick. I didn't even touch the wine.'

'Sure.' She winks at me. 'So, how is your love life, now?'

I groan.

'You should come to one of my speed dating nights.'

'You run speed dating as well?'

'Yes, at the Valley.'

'That would be interesting.'

'It is. Kaden, a lot of couples send me wedding invitations.'

Julie and I have both had a little too much to drink when we walk the two kilometres back to her apartment. She's already made me a nest for the night, in the corner next to the computer, a thick pile of sheets and a European pillow. I can tell this is where her Christmas tree stood, as there is a pine needle wedged in the floorboards. Julie mumbles something comforting before she turns off the light and I hold onto my toes and sleep.

On Thursday I follow Milligan into the sun, and we walk down to where the company's wharf is. It's on the other side of the island from the commercial jetty. My boat, or the boat I'll be using, hangs by itself at the end of the row; it's the one with the dent in the side. The outside is the same colour as a coconut. It is old and rusty, and when Milligan helps me on and in it, my legs wobble a bit too much, enough for him to look at me and ask if I'm okay. The sea is nauseatingly close, a blue too bright, the smell of salt and fish guts. I sit up, cross my legs. I watch Milligan's every move, as I know he's only going to show me once. I watch him put on sunscreen.

'Here, have some,' he says.

'No, I'm not bothered.'

'You should. Here— '

'I don't burn,' I say, looking down at my arms.

He looks at me, and I shrug and take the tube off him and lather my skin a little.

Milligan has drawn me a 'map' on the back of a burger wrapper. He's already said that the company gets burgers delivered every Friday lunch and I have to put my order in with Sophie.

His sketch shows Russell Island as a large curve, an open mouth that takes up half the page. Off it are the three small jagged islands. He has numbered them, 1, 2, 3. The number 4 is marked on Russell Island, but further down than where we are.

'So, simple, yes? After you've established a rapport this will be your routine. First thing you go out to 1. You give them their formula. You communicate with them on their daily needs. Then you move on to 2, 3 and 4. Same thing. Then in the middle of the day you have your rest, have your lunch, catch up with any things that need doing. This won't be much at the start, but trust me, you'll learn to use this time wisely. Then, in the afternoon, you pick up the formulas, from 1, 2, 3 and 4, take them back to base and to the lab for refilling.'

'Got it,' I say.

'I'm giving you free rein on this, which means you don't have to report back to me every day, only where there are negotiations that need to be run past me. But it is five weeks. That's how long you've got to get all of them out of the way, preferably onto Russell. So that's what you've got to be telling yourself, all the time. Five weeks.'

As I watch Milligan steer the boat I realise, for the first time, this is not going to be easy physically. Milligan was swearing and sweating securing the boat every time we reached an isle, and he doesn't seem unfit to me. The trip was repetitive, and numbing, and the sun made it harder to endure. I'd already finished my water by the time we reached the second point. Out on the water, I didn't really get a chance to meet any of them. As we passed each group, Milligan would yell out a greeting, and introduce me. He seems very uncomfortable with the plantpeople. I can't get over how much they look like us when they're talking to each other. Especially the younger ones.

★

After I've recovered from the day, in the cool of the late afternoon, I walk to the beach. Even though Russell is covered in sand, there is only one real beach, a few paces from the jetty. It seems to be a 'thing' at this time of day, the residents, my neighbours, go to Jim's store and buy something greasy, then go sit on the lumpy beach and watch the waves. A lot of them also go into the water, bodysurf or just satisfy their ankles. They play in the sand, and a few throw a cricket ball back and forth to each other. They behave like children, in a place where there are few, if any children.

Otherwise I don't see much of the neighbours. There is a guy with a pick-up truck that sometimes drives past and asks if I need a lift, but that's it.

I sit for a while up on the rock and eat a Portuguese custard tart out of the soft paper serviette I wrapped it in from Jim's shop. It tastes so fresh. Soon I grow tired of watching the water. It is too like the hours I spent out on it today. I'm not ready to go home, though. Home is getting lonely and I know I'll spend the remaining hours before I go to sleep in insignificant ways, cleaning or doing crossword puzzles on the bed. I slip off my boots and stand, stamping my feet into the sand and seeing the prints I make. I'm facing away from the water, with the feel of the last sunlight on my lower back. Then I walk away from the people towards a path that goes around the corner. The sand feels good on my feet. This path is curious and around the bend it opens onto another small beach, which at present holds no people. There is a short, disused jetty in the water. I walk towards it, this small beach, and realise I can see the mainland from here, a great black blur. The sand is more shelly and rocky, and there are blue blobs dotted along the water's edge. I don't think I should go near them.

The jetty is rotting and falling apart before my eyes. I am drawn closer to it. The wood catches the sun's glint and sparkles. I walk into the water and stand beneath it, touching the wood at head height.

When I walk back onto the sand I stop for a moment. My foot is burning. I turn it over and see a red circle on the sole. I hold it, try to walk on it. I manage for a while before it's too painful. I hobble back into the sea and feel the water rush against my foot. The water is nice and cool, but it doesn't bring any relief. I quickly get out. I sit on the sand and wince and try to think about what to do. The red on the sole of my foot has spread. I wonder how long I will sit here until it gets better.

I see a plantperson come around the corner, in the far line of my vision. My heart bubbles a bit with hope. My thoughts bump up against each other. I don't know whether I should put up a red flag or just sit here and hope they come to me. Maybe I don't need their help, anyway. Maybe they can't help me.

I think the pain is getting worse. I look again at my foot, and try not to be alarmed when I see red lines stretching across the skin, almost to the top of my foot.

Then I realise the plantperson is Larapinta. It is Larapinta and the way I am sitting, there's no way she wouldn't figure it out.

'Blue bottle?' she says, getting near.

I nod. 'I put some water on it.'

'Seawater?'

I nod.

'That made it worse?' She comes by me. She's an awkward tangle of roots and limbs and when she walks she creaks like an old stair railing. 'You need fresh water. Which foot is it?'

I hesitate before showing her. If she was a human, Julie or somebody, she would tell me I'm an idiot. Make me feel like a total newbie who shouldn't be walking around the island unsupervised. What kind of Aboriginal person are you? Can't survive taking your shoes off.

But she's not human, so I feel better. My breathing slows. She does her trick again. I haven't yet been able to believe it. She extracts the saltwater out of my skin with her middle fingertip and then releases a flow of freshwater; just the first drop makes it better. The saltiness is out.

I get up and hobble around and she gets me to sit on the old piece of wood, the jetty, without having my feet in the water.

'Thank you so much,' I say.

'You're welcome,' she says.

'Lucky you were here.'

'This is where I stay most nights.' She motions to where she's come from. We sit in silence. It's getting dark.

'You think you can walk now?'

I nod and she helps me up.

'Larapinta?'

She looks up.

I don't want to be rude but I say, 'What would you say you are? And where do you come from?'

She looks at me. 'Can you answer that about yourself?'

'I guess not.'

'For us it is the same.'

'Have you always been here?'

'Yes.'

'Have you ever been stung?'

'It's probable.'

'You don't feel pain?'

'Not that sort of pain.'

'What kind?'

'When I'm away from sunlight. When I see others ripped. But not death. Death doesn't affect me.'

We talk a little more as she walks me back along the sandy path and to the main beach. The day has faded red in the sunset. We decide we won't talk about the politics. What side we're on.

In the morning I pick up the formula from the lab and take the boat out by myself. On the first islet I see both Larapinta and Hinter, whom I have been introduced to. Hinter is very different to Larapinta. I observe the smaller plantpeople next to them, half the height but still the same width. They are a community with no hierarchy of age or gender. They stand in a row, long and thin figures. They make the sky seem pale and the individual seem insignificant.

When I approach to give them the formula, they greet me in a distracted sort of way, like they're half there. Names do not seem of significance; they don't bother with mine or their own. They only seem of relevance when they need something from the human world, like Larapinta does. She needs her books. And I don't know what Hinter needs, but he is always at the Centre, too. When I ask Larapinta where she got her name, she said it was the name of the scientist's daughter. I say it's better than a number. She puts her head to the side and says she likes numbers. I can't help but laugh at the thought of her being into numerology, believing in it. But who am I to judge, I think later when I'm back at home and all is quiet in the night. I don't believe in anything.

You should see the way they walk through water. Their heads like a tangling piece of reed. And you'll look closer and see their shoulders swing back and forth like some smooth stroke and it's frightening.

It's a short stretch from the bank to each island. It takes me about ten minutes to line the boat out and reach the other side. Yet going back and forth this short distance all day sometimes gives me a feeling of dizziness, like I can't remember which bank is which, and all the edges, the coastal shrubbery, look the same. And the distances add up.

Early in the day, while I'm on the water, the time seems to go really slow, and my thoughts cramp. I'm bored and anxious, like when I worked at the biscuit factory. But after a while, the tasks on the water become relaxing and I find myself thinking of Dad, and other things. Maybe I can find some sort of peace with myself out here.

Larapinta offers to accompany me. I try not to show my surprise to her when, at the end of the delivery round to each island, all plantpeople have taken the formula, every single one of them. She did say to trust them, that things would run smoothly. I help the plantpeople with the buckets, filling the containers with water from the sea.

When the formula buckets are ready I watch the plant-people in fascination as their feet change, gain curve and lose their definition, transform into roots. They move their roots into the bucket and roll their heads back.

'How long?' I mouth to Larapinta.

'Until you come back. After the sun is at its highest.'

I wait until we are further away and back into the boat before I speak privately to her. I've noticed that Larapinta hasn't taken her own formula yet.

'What does it feel like?'

'Digesting.'

When we're moving, she curls herself up between the stern of the boat and the seat, and I ask her more than once if she's comfortable where she is or if she would like to move.

She just looks at me. I think she would be amused by me if she could be amused.

'It's hard, isn't it?' she asks as we make our second journey across the stretch of water to the next island and secure the boat.

I look at her. 'Are you going to tell me the person before me didn't last a week on the job?'

'There was no one before you,' Larapinta replies.

When I see her take the formula, her roots soaking in the bucket, I ask her if she likes it.

She answers: 'It keeps the soapberry bugs away. They usually come in this season.'

'Why do you like to come in the boat with me? Not that I mind, you're a big help.'

'I have time to myself.' She's on her e-reader again.

After a week I am getting fit from rowing, my arms are built and tanned. My skin, which was always quite brown, the colour white people are when they are really tanned, is darker. My legs and arms and feet are the colour of wood, though my face is red and blotchy and when Milligan sees me he tells me I should be wearing the sunscreen.

My mother would tell me, too. She burnt from getting the newspaper off the porch stairs. She had a melanoma cut out of her hand. But when I was little, Dad and I lived off the sun. We spent the whole day in the fields. Never in the shade. And I lost the wide-brimmed hats my mother bought me on purpose.

My shoulders are always tight. I usually prop up an elbow on the side of the boat and scrunch up the hair that falls on my forehead.

My body is mostly covered in scratches from the reeds and bites, I think they're mosquitoes. The next time I'm in the office I ask Milligan for some repellent. He just shrugs and says that eventually, when my body is covered in bites, even my arse, and the sandflies try to bite the bites, they will stop and I will be immune. I have a feeling I should have asked Sophie instead.

I get some spray from Jim's shop on the way home and put it in my boat bag. I also allow myself the same treat after each day's work. The creamy custard tarts from the kiosk are unbelievable. I have usually finished one before I reach my front door.

My knots are getting quite good. It was Larapinta that showed me how to do them. The way she talks is like a computer program, always in stages. She's been hanging around me too much already, though – sometimes she'll say one of my expressions, and roll her words out more casually.

When I tell her about it she says she has to do more reading. She is determined to learn *casual English*. Maybe I'm a bit determined to figure her out – well, at least plant-people in general.

I exhaust myself on the boat, especially when Larapinta is not available to help me. I need to be faster. At night I do crunches on the bed until I can feel my dinner.

I'm always interested in what Larapinta's reading. Yesterday it was Mills & Boon. Today it is the encyclopaedia, she's up to volume M. She reads unbelievably fast, absorbs the words, though I wonder if they hold any meaning for her. I want to tell her there's not much point knowing every-thing, when you don't know one thing well.

I haven't been able to stop staring at her. I know she's not a freak show, believe me. I watch her extract water from her hands. It doesn't get old. She tells me that she will grow flowers soon. She points out one of the sandplants on the second island. When we are closer, I see that he or she indeed has flowers growing on their body.

She liked a scarf I was wearing, the flowing green one my mother bought me for Christmas, so I gave it to her. It sits on her shoulders and waltzes in the wind. I tell her it suits her.

I never see anything in the water. Only the occasional brown swarm of catfish. Larapinta told me of the dugong she saw one day behind the boat shed, she was holding one of the plantchildren, walking with her in the sandy enclave.

'What was it like?'

'It was like seeing a shooting star in the sky.'

'You've been reading too much romance,' I say. 'Stick to the encyclopaedias.'

It's the second Friday – burger day in the office. After I go out in the morning, I take the boat back to the mainland around 12 p.m. and walk up the sand to the office.

Everyone is there, crowding around in Milligan's office, as there is no kitchen, and I realise I still haven't met half of these people, my coworkers. They are a combination of office workers and scientists. I see the young man who gives me the formula every morning and go stand next to him in the corner. Sophie passes me my burger. I'm surprised it's still warm.

'So you got the satay tofu one, too, hey?' the young botanist says to me.

I nod. From his eagerness, he seems not to know anyone either.

'How are the specimens taking to the formula?' he asks.

'Yeah, no problems,' I say.

'Good. Hopefully that stays the same when the dosage changes.'

'The dosage changes?' Milligan didn't tell me about this.

'Oh well, it's a gradual increase in the percentage of ... chlorine ... this will make them more docile ...'

I look at him and realise my mouth is hanging open and my reaction is showing.

'Are the plantpeople aware of this? This changed formula?'

He shrugs and looks across at Milligan. 'Not entirely. I don't think you should be discussing it with them.'

'I feel it's part of my job. It's ethical.'

He snorts. 'We're talking about plants here.'

'They're not just plants, you must know that.'

'They're not entirely human, though, are they? Not close. We've been having these debates for years. About scientific testing on animals for medical research. At the end of the day, we have to put humans first.'

'So that's science? Science is biased to the human race? This is sounding like social Darwinism, like the twisted justification of treating black people worse because of their race and skin colour.'

He's looking pained. 'I'd keep it quiet, if I were you. Milligan's just over there.'

I cross my arms over my chest. My first job, in the biscuit factory, was when I was in high school. I've developed a robust operational style – and am always described as hard-working. I don't usually let people get me off course.

He continues in a reasoned voice. 'Look, obviously we're from different schools of thought. But as long as we keep doing our individual *jobs*, we'll be fine.'

Larapinta touched me. It was an accident, I think. A miscalculation. But how does a plant miscalculate? A plant is a subject of environment.

I tell her about the pool I used to swim every afternoon. Larapinta, with her usual bluntness, asks why I don't swim in the sea. I shrug, and don't have an answer. Larapinta tells me she'll take me out when the tide is low.

We find ourselves talking about gender. We are of two different societies. She asks me if I feel like a woman, even though I have short hair. I tell her that hair is the least of it. She asks me about my Aboriginal identity. I tell her that it is easy to pretend that I am someone else, but I don't want to pretend.

'And your sexual identity?' She is really in the mood for grilling me.

'Queer, I guess.' I say. 'I know it's an old-fashioned word ...'

'That is fine. I do not know the common usage of words. They are bricks, aren't they?'

'Some words are loaded,' I continue. 'Will always be loaded.'

'I must return to my reading,' she says.

She is brushing up against me in the dinghy again. Surprisingly, her prickly skin doesn't irritate mine. I have found that some plants thrive on neglect. I try to push her away but she comes at me with the power of the bloom.

She is not human, so she can stare until her eyes tear up and it doesn't mean anything.

'I've been thinking about you,' she says after my third week on the job. We are at our favourite spot, by the derelict jetty, my shoes off and my feet dangling over, the storm clouds eating away at the last light in the sky.

'You don't think,' I say. 'It's just processes.'

'I have been thinking ... a lot. I have enough intelligence; what I'm lacking is the emotional intelligence ... But I think we do have what you call a "sparkle".'

'It's a spark. It's not a fucking *sparkle*.'

She's not taken aback at my outburst. 'Finally. A political statement.'

I shift my body and our shoulders brush. We don't find each other. Then I feel her foot tangle around mine and she puts her arm around me.

'Two worlds?'

'I don't know if ...' I move away. 'You're not ...' I can't offend her.

'What you expected?' She's getting used to the patterns of speech. 'Humans never see what's coming. Everything is seasonal, cyclical, dependent on environment and weather conditions. Would I love you in the winter, when my toes are frost? Would I love you in the summer, when the wind comes tumbling on me?'

To understand, I give myself the first question. What is a plant? A plant is a living organism. A plant has cell walls with cellulose and characteristically they obtain most of their energy through sunlight. Plants provide most of the world's molecular energy and are the basis of most of the world's ecologies, especially on land. Plants are one of the two main groups into which all living things have been traditionally divided; the other is animals. The division goes back at least as far as Aristotle, who distinguished between plants which generally do not move, and animals which often are mobile to catch their food.

The second question is harder. It is: What is a human?

When I walk the beach at night the sandplants are folded. Larapinta is in the line. Her chin is tucked, her arms by her sides. They look like scarecrows standing there under the moon. I don't tell Larapinta how near I am to the jetty if she should need a place to rest her head.

I remember a conversation I had with Milligan, early on. He cleared his throat and I looked seriously at him.

'Kaden, it's come to my attention, through research, that as these sandplants can closely resemble us and mimic our behaviour – well, some people in close proximity can find themselves getting quite attached. Now that's fine, in the same way that of course we get attached to our cat or dog, maybe even to our mango tree that's been in the backyard for a few generations. But there have been cases of sexual attraction. Some lost souls. Now, strictly off the record here, as a male I find, say, Larapinta, slightly of an attractive quality, it's natural, she's more human-like than the others in the way she looks. And females may feel the same way about Hinter. But it is unnatural if you take it that couple of steps further.

The government has recognised the danger – it is, of course, illegal to be in any way romantically involved with them. There was a fellow who, I won't go into details, he got himself *engaged* with one of them, and hurt himself quite badly. It was unnatural and not possible.

I'm just letting you know as a Cultural Liaison Officer, mediator between them and us, to keep an eye out for those sort of things going on. You're a little naive; I know such things might seem strange and unlikely to you, but it can happen. It could have deadly effects.'

I don't think Milligan knows, in our culture, *deadly* means really good. I decided not to tell him that.

I've been taking notes in the field. About the tides, the winds and how many strokes it takes me to get to each isle on the belt.

I'm getting better. My hands no longer blister. When Larapinta is in the boat the time goes faster. I can get swept into a conversation about the geography and don't notice my arms clenching back and forth until I'm at the bank.

My hair's getting long. I'm thinking of getting it cut next time I'm on the mainland. Sometimes I forget a band or a tie when I'm out on the boat, and it cuts into my face like a whip.

I've been going for longer walks lately. I tell myself it's to stretch out my legs after all those hours on the boat, but really it's because of the feeling of being cramped up on the island. I know it too well. It takes nineteen minutes to walk the whole island.

It's about time I go see my mother, eat cold macaroni in the kitchen I grew up in. She always brushes back my unkempt fringe, and she'll dig out a batch of old photos, a birthday card I made my father. Why does she do it? I don't cry anymore. I can talk about my father without crying.

Mum still thinks that pasta is my favourite thing ever. To be fair, I probably don't know her as well as I think I do either, not anymore. She has a whole other life in the weeks, sometimes months I don't see her.

After Dad died, Mum and I were inseparable for a while. She even got a job at my school. The thing is, I was always closer to Dad, and that didn't change, even after he was dead. My mother no doubt couldn't understand it, it probably frustrated her a little bit, as when he was alive, Dad wasn't around. He was always in the studio he shared with his brothers, or with family, or travelling for or with his art.

We stand on the second isle and I pass out the formula, like I do every morning. I watch Larapinta kissing a seedling's head, brushing the pillow-like fronds of hair out of his eyes. I like the seedlings, babies, really they are a bundle of brown, often held by the others.

Larapinta doesn't wait for the quiet moments to ask her usual odd questions. 'What is it like to menstruate?'

I shrug and no longer hesitate, used to her quirkiness. 'Ah. I guess it's not too bad. I don't mind it. It's part of being a woman. Damn expensive, though. All that tax. Thought President Sparkle would have done something about it.'

'Are you menstruating now?' Larapinta asks.

'I am due to.'

'Does it affect your sexual activity?'

'No, not really.'

'Good,' she says, and she *winks*.

She's letting me know she wants to try something out. We were talking about how the bay is known for its abundance of seafood. Everywhere, a fisherman's dream. She talks low to me, tells me I should invite her to spend the afternoon and we'll cook a fresh catch, eat together.

She doesn't eat, but she'd like to try for me, even just pretend. I look at her mouth, red and ripe as a baby animal's.

'Neither of us know how to fish, though,' I say, even though I shouldn't humour her.

'We'll get a bottle of nice wine.'

'Are you talking about seduction?' A thought comes to my head. I'm being seduced by a plant. 'It's foolish, Larapinta.'

She looks back down at her e-reader.

I continue. 'I can't, professionally. Personally as well. We need to stick in our own corners.'

I'm glad she can't judge me. I'm afraid she can see into me.

Julie has already ordered my regular, the lasagne and chips. She's gotten herself a salad. She's on a diet. 'Not going too well,' she says about it. 'The other day I picked up a donut. I wish I had the energy I used to. I want to play tennis again.'

'You're looking healthy to me.' I look at her clear olive skin, her white teeth. Electric blue eyes: contacts.

She reaches for the dressing. I don't tell her about Larapinta. I don't know how she'd react about me getting along with a plantperson. Julie already thinks I'm anti-social.

A band plays in the corner. There are two young fellas playing together. One main singer with a sweet voice, tall and wearing a grey beanie. The other man sits on a drum and plays it; he's a shorter, older fella. He sings in some songs, a quick, direct style, almost like a rap. Julie says the second singer is awful. I don't know, maybe I've been hanging out too much with Larapinta, but I don't have a taste filter. I think they're both good at what they do. If you want to do a five-minute solo imitating the sound of a train in a tunnel, that's okay.

Because of the music, Julie makes us move to the back. She talks a bit more about Sparkle. When she was in Sydney, Julie was heavily involved in the art scene, and also campaigning for our people. What my mum says about Julie when she's tired is that Julie uses her looks to get what she wants. Julie did have a flash job down in Sydney, but she worked hard for it, I know she did.

Sometime during the night Julie talks about the heavy pay cut she took for her new job in Brisbane. She's losing money as she still hasn't yet found a buyer for her place in Sydney. 'I should get into painting,' Julie jokes. 'All I have to do is a few brown dots and our totem.'

'What's our totem?' I ask her.

'Oh, come on, you know that,' Julie says. She takes a sip. 'It's a dugong.'

It is instinctive; I've had too much to drink. I get off the ferry in the middle of the night and go to the beach and lie down. When I wake up I feel the hot sand press against my cheek and my thoughts immediately go to Larapinta. I find myself imagining the tart taste of her mouth. She comes up too often, in my dreams and in waking, on my afternoon walks and in the cold morning air. She is deliberate in the way she talks to me. I am a curiosity she wants to explore. I'm sure if it was someone else it would be the same to her. I just happen to be here, in a boat with her seven hours a day.

★

In the afternoon, Larapinta takes me to the place she saw the dugong, past the second sandy embankment where she helped me when I got stung by the bluebottle, and up an incline. We stand there stiffly. I see boats on the clear water. I see the lazy shape of turtles. I don't see a dugong.

'Maybe she has gone home,' she says. What a strange statement to come from something like her.

For a tiny moment when we are standing there and the breeze is lifting, it rains lightly. Just a thin veil over the view. I can hardly even feel the raindrops.

Soon it is dark and she pulls on my arm and asks if she can follow me home. I ask for a reason and she answers: 'I want to be with you so we can do what is private.' Then she leans close to my ear and utters '*private*' again. My blush stops me from saying anything at all and I just walk numbly to my street and open both doors of my house.

We step inside and turn to each other and I realise she is the same height and it would not be difficult to kiss her.

I let her in my mouth. What will this experiment hold for her – what will she find in the flesh of my tongue, the crest of my lips? What will I discover in this uncharted experience? How much of what it means to be human will sway deep in my mind like a ship. I see her eyes are open, those green unhuman eyes, watching, looking at me, but not. Her mouth is alive. I suck on her bottom lip, surrender my teeth. She makes a noise that I could only interpret as arousal but in the weeks I've known her I've never heard her display in utterance. To feel she is human now is a lie, I must be with who she is. I feel her mind crackle on mine as our foreheads touch, I feel what is between her eyes. We lie down on the bed and she takes off my boots. Her hands are my body temperature. We embrace each other, cradle the warmth between us.

Her shoulder connects, her arm loops into mine. I feel the weight of my own arousal, the humming in my breast. She doesn't tire, her breathing remains steady. In the dark of the room, her shadow enclosed into mine, she could be anything.

While we rest I contemplate telling her this is my first time in quite a while. To try and explain the reason why my knees shook, why there were tears of confusion on my face. I struggle to get the words out and wait for her reply.

'Everything is new for me,' she says. 'I am renewal.'

Surprised by her response, I look at her.

'I was made to adapt,' she says.

'Adapt? Can you adapt to love?'

'I already have,' she says. She shows me her flowers, one on each fingertip of her right hand. Red, with a bit of yellow. No more than a millimetre.

I've had bosses like him before. Authorial, edgy, say what they think without worrying about criticism.

I've mostly stayed out of their way.

Milligan doesn't micro-manage me, but there is an expectancy that I go to see him every day, smile and say hello, and nod politely while he rants about the budget and reports. Milligan tells me some nasty truths about the Gov, and the more switched-on I become, the more I am uncomfortable. I realise how naive I was before coming here.

When he talks about the sandplants he sometimes refers to them as 'weeds': 'How you handling the weeds?' he says.

I don't say much.

'One week, you got left. You can go home if you're pussy.'

'Excuse me?' I say.

He laughs.

I walked down George Street today. There was some big protest going on outside parliament house. Lots of Murris around. Stupidly, I looked for my uncle in the crowd. I got closer and stood in the background, watching the group of protesters move back and forth like chess pieces, not getting too close to the police watching from the bays.

There were whole families and an even mix of men and women. Mostly in black T-shirts.

One sign facing me said, *The cultural displacement continues!*

I looked up at the windows of the tall building. President Sparkle wouldn't be here, she was never here. She would be in Sydney or on the other side of the world. So why were these people here now? Then I realised that today was the date. By an online 'enrolment', Aboriginal people could sign up to live on Australia2. The government would decide whether the individuals met the Confirmation criteria, and assign them a block of land.

It had come up so many times in the office, but I was used to hearing it from the other end, the guvvie buzzwords and contractions.

What I was feeling from the crowd was so … *raw* that I felt my shoulders pull together and my stomach drop.

As much as the government thought they did, as much as Sparkle thought they did, these people didn't want to live in this new 'country'. They didn't want Australia2. I wanted to go up to them, introduce myself, feel their feeling. Tell them I'm Murri, too, even though I don't really look it.

I did end up talking to someone, a man who reminded me of my uncle, though he would be a decade younger.

'You're Marvin's daughter, aren't you?' he said, coming alongside my shoulder.

'Yes, how do you know?' I said.

'I used to know your dad quite well, and he would bring you along to barbecues and things.' He changed his stance to greet me. 'I'm Hugo.'

Hugh Ngo. The artist. He must have seen my half-look of recognition because he said, 'Your dad and I, and your uncles and a few others, we were all at Yarapi for a while. Your dad was the best, I really think so. His work was admired on a global scale.'

I felt that nervousness, that reluctance I felt when someone spoke about my dad and his art. I had made a decision as a teenager that I didn't want anything to do with the crowd, the painters, the appraisers, the gallery workers. I didn't bother with it. What did it matter, Dad was gone.

'When we lost your dad, it shocked a lot of us into action. We had to stop their control of our art.'

'But you haven't,' I blurted. 'It's still the same.'

He shook his head. 'I don't make art for galleries. Or for money. I make art that speaks the truth.'

★

I'm out on the boat. It is 6 a.m. Early. I keep checking my watch. My hair is still wet at the ends from my morning shower. I'm not stopping at the smaller islands; I am powering onward.

By now I'm good at steering the boat. I wouldn't have done this a few weeks ago, but now I'm confident. Yesterday, while I was in the city, I looked at maps in the library. I found the reference desk and asked them where their map collection was. I found a map of the Moreton Bay islands, and located Ki. I did the calculations to figure out how I would navigate there. I was used to making short and direct journeys. To get to Ki involved dribbling through a maze of sandbanks and little islands like the ones the plant-people lived on. Then a long stretch out, which I was most worried about.

I don't pass any other boats. When I do see Ki, I'm struck by how big it is. I know it is almost as big as Russell, but it's more of a thin shape. Approaching the evacuated island, I slow the boat and find a little groove. There is a security guard there. Pointing with my chin, I show him the pass around my neck. He gives me a half-look and accepts with his eyes. I get out of the boat and suddenly feel exposed. Security everywhere, strolling lines like wolves in uniforms.

I make my way up a small hill and reach the treeline. It is a strange feeling. Other people may see the she-oaks and the sandy-coloured boulder with the skink on it. They might notice the air as quiet and crisp and the female magpie hopping on the grass, but I see something else, I feel something else.

I walk on. There is a light on in one of the houses across the park and I think about the house my dad used to live in, then further back to when it wasn't a house, when the old people used to walk here bare-footed. I even take off my shoes and find a dark place under the shade of a wattle tree where I don't think the workers will hear me, and I shout – a brisk guttural bark – cut off, because I pull back when I think about them finding me.

The light on is a curiosity. Maybe someone forgot to turn off the lights before they evacuated. It is orange, like the bulb is high-voltage.

I find a vantage point where I can see most of the island and the sea stretched around it. I stay there as long as I can, but what can I do? It's a dying place, more or less. The beauty is dying – all around – the industry is strangling it. The wires they are putting under the sea and the water they will pump away will destroy all of this.

There is a groping sense of relief that I feel something: for this place, in this place. My country. My dad's country. But this relief quickly turns into a bitter sense of loss and regret, almost self-loathing in despair.

Later that day as I'm rowing up the island, close to the dock, I overhear an animated conversation. Two voices. I approach hesitantly. Larapinta is talking to Hinter, their backs to me. They are speaking in language. It sounds like Indigenous language. Larapinta is singing. Her voice is a rush in my ears. I cling to the reeds. When the boat drifts further forward and Larapinta sees me she stops. I try to make sense of what I've just witnessed.

At first we speak to each other like the other night didn't happen. Though she carries her weight around me. I want to question her about the language and what she was singing, but she chooses this moment to let her shoulder clip mine, and her lips to brush against my hair.

I look at the others, who aren't watching. I ask her if she's coming in the boat.

'Not today.' She keeps looking over at Hinter and the others. I think sometimes they communicate telepathically. I think she doesn't want me to know something. I don't know what's happened.

When, after my shift, I go back to the island and Larapinta is not there, I suddenly feel this furious rush; I had wanted to ask her about the language. I pick at the dirt under my fingernails and wait awhile, but she doesn't show.

Milligan has made me a coffee. Normally it would look like a nice gesture, but Milligan's sadistic. I don't usually drink coffee anyway, it makes me anxious. As I predicted, it wasn't an onya meeting. He started off with saying he didn't see any progress with me.

'You're distracted. What is it? You can tell me,' he said. 'You're slipping off the plate, Kaden.'

I tried to reason that everything was fine.

'If it's them taking the formula, we can get Jack out there with you.'

'They're taking their formula,' I lied.

I haven't been going out regularly since last week, and I don't give them the formula in the way I used to. I talked to Larapinta, I told her about the increase of chlorine and she said they had been feeling a difference since taking it. Larapinta and the others worked out for themselves it was a trick; they agreed they didn't want it. They have started to wean themselves off it gradually. I've been covering it up, tossing the remainder in the sea and watching the dark streak it leaves. From talking to Jack in the lab, I know the shit would eventually kill them, and they've been developing another, more vicious substance, that will kill them faster.

Milligan says, 'I know you're connecting with them. But you're putting it ahead of your job, it's distracting you. I hired you because I thought you could handle the pressure. People trust you. You make them listen.'

I had to stop myself from crying. I knew I could easily walk out of there, walk off the job, take it from there. The coffee was weak, it tasted like soap suds. I let the meeting draw to a natural close, let Milligan know he had made his message clear, and then I left for the day.

My dad gave me a language name. Kaden means orchid. Dad would paint flowers when he wasn't painting dots. He never stopped. It was always the next one. But sometimes he gave himself the time to do the flowers. Maybe a Sunday afternoon, I was home and he was in the backyard. Mum said she wanted to call me Sylvia, Dad had won after a best-out-of-five in dominoes, four to one. I'd like to think my fate was more than just chance. Why did Dad have to name me in a language I don't know? It was insult to injury. Julie says that her dad speaks a little of their grandmother's language to her. I wonder if my dad would have, or did.

From the art, Dad's estate, Mum and I have enough money to live comfortably, with no worries. Though why would Mum move from our family house, and why would I not try to make a decent career for myself?

Dad was already pretty well known in the Brisbane scene for his glasswork before Tanya Sparkle became President. He had a few paintings showcased in a little New Farm gallery when an art critic tapped him on the shoulder and told him that's where the money was. Just around when all those reforms took place, the government set up Yarapi, and they enlisted Dad straightaway. Dad and my uncles must have thought it was a good thing at the time, Brisbane's first Aboriginal art gallery. But it was only the start of things, here and around the country. It was a factory. They had the artists working twelve hours a day to produce. And the art didn't belong to them, not at the end of the day. The money started rolling in and Dad's art was commissioned every-where – they wanted his art in parliament house and on planes and footy shirts. I watched him wade into the public side of things, the interviews, the appearances. It wore him down pretty quickly, the expectations. A few years later they also started the generational thing. The children of this generation of artists were worth a lot, like the offspring of a racehorse.

There was one summer where Dad sold his first million-dollar painting to buyers in Russia and went from one side of the country to the next talking about art he had no passion for, art that was supposedly his cultural expres-sion but had become something that ate at him. That was the summer we lost him. A few days after he came home,

Mum found him in the bath, fully dressed. An overdose, the doctors said.

By the afternoon I'm sitting next to Julie at the bar and know she's also thinking about her father. Our fathers were best friends, and family men. Julie reveals to me her times spent with her dad on Ki when he told her things – like that the old people who have gone are still in the land.

She has admitted to me the real reason she moved back home was her dad is dying. It is a cancer he got from inhaling paint fumes in those gallery spaces.

'How long does Uncle have?' I say, quietly shaken, even though he's been poorly on and off. I put my arms around her and it is a natural thing, we know each other enough for this now.

'We're not sure. Maybe six months. Maybe more.' She wipes the tears from her eyes. 'Hey, it was your mum, you know.'

'What do you mean?' I say.

'It was your mum who stopped them making me an artist. Enlisting me. She protected me from them. The agents and the suppliers. And I think she did the same for you.'

I nod, and look at the screen above my head, the news headlines flashing in red.

'God, Tanya Sparkle,' Julie says. 'Enough is enough.'

I drink my cider. Julie has a fancy-looking mocktail. We're close enough to exchange smells: her, mint and paw-paw lotion – me, sweat and burnt wood.

'We're fighting them,' Julie says.

'What?'

She blinks her blue eyes again like she regrets her words. 'My dad. Uncle Theo. All of us mob.'

'Why didn't you tell me?'

'Because you're the government,' Julie says. 'Who you work for.'

'I'm family,' I say. 'I'm not one of them.'

Julie puts her hand down hard on my shoulder. 'I know.'

'What are you going to do?' I ask.

Julie turns around, scours the other people, as if worried they will hear us. 'Not here. Come on.' She drags her clutch off the table.

'Where are we going?'

She holds out her hand for me. 'Are you coming? Dad's expecting you.'

Her car is parked just around the corner in a little alleyway. Julie drives us up the highway to Caboolture. When we arrive, Julie walks me to the gate and keeps me at the letterbox. She goes in and a minute later I see him at the doorway.

He is wearing pyjamas and slippers. There is a gap between his teeth you could slide a yo-yo in, and the sun shines through. His hair is unexpectedly silver. Behind him Julie gives a nod of her head and I stutter forward, suddenly aware of the nerves fuzzing my legs.

We greet each other and he kisses my cheek, 'So nice to see you, niece.'

Inside he has a television on; I haven't seen one for years. He has been watching one of the *Alien* movies. We sit down on the couch. We catch up on the last few years of our lives.

I don't ask him about his health, and he seems to make a conscious decision not to talk about it either.

He coughs. 'Julie tells me where you work.'

I look down, not sure on how to answer. Is he disappointed in me?

'The *sandplants*,' he says. 'Them mob.'

I lift my eyes from the movie and look at him, then Julie. 'I heard them speaking language.'

Uncle looks directly at me and speaks naturally in the same language, and I feel goosebumps up my arm. 'Jangigir,' he says then.

I stumble over my words. 'Are they ... Indigenous?'

'They are our old people. Spirits. Something happened when the dugai brought the sea up. They rose with it.'

I look over at Julie.

My uncle continues. 'Their knowledge goes back, big time, bub. They've helped us piece back our language. And they're going to help us stop this—' He points to the television, which has changed to the news, Australia2 the lead story once again. Tanya Sparkle's red face in close-up.

'We are going to fight. We are the Traditional Owners. We're going to secure our islands so they can't be harmed. Starting with Ki.'

I feel a strong flutter in my gut.

'They want us to be self-governed. But we can't end up like the TSI mob.' He pauses to clear his throat. 'They want to segregate us. Cast us out for good. Everything that this President has done has drifted us – blackfellas and whitefellas – further apart.'

Julie touches his arm. 'How about I make us some tea. Kaden probably doesn't want to hear this all at once.'

'She needs to hear it. She is one of us.' He coughs.

His phone rings and Julie picks it up off the mantelpiece. 'It's Hinter,' she says, not answering it.

'Tell Hinter to call back – Kaden is here.'

'Hinter? How are they part of it?'

Uncle says, 'they are our numbers.'

'And they're happy, they're happy to do that?' I say.

He nods. 'Of course.'

I realise that they are the sacrifice.

'We're taking back the islands. Ki first. Larapinta will call them at nightfall,' he says.

I feel a pang at her name. Why didn't she tell me?

He continues. 'We need you to log in, put a temporary roadblock on the surveillance.'

'So this is what it is.' I look over at Julie suddenly. 'You put me up to this, didn't you? It's all been leading to this.'

'Kaden.' Julie tries to calm me.

'Don't.' And I wrestle out of there with tears on my shirt collar.

My stomach is empty. I feel I will never eat again. I catch a cab to my mother's house. Somehow she knows what I need. Space. In the dark of my old room.

They want to kill them. Send them out as warriors. I won't be part of it. They had this perfect plan, with me as the pawn. My own family. Why didn't they show any interest in me before? Only when they wanted something. For so long I'd been alone with all these questions about who I was and I hadn't even realised how much I was hurting. I was empty. Not able to connect with anyone. And then, under the strange, intense circumstances, I was drawn to Larapinta; somehow she had understood me, she made me want more for myself. And now I would lose her.

I let the evening slip, and then the next morning, knowing full well I've missed work. My mother leaves me a fruit and nut bagel, toasted and spread, by the door. Next time she comes she gives me coffee with cream stirred in. I take the coffee, but apologise about the bagel, still on the plate.

My mother gives me one of her T-shirts. White, it stretches when I pull it over my head and is too tight across my breasts. I hear her humming to herself above the radio advertisements as she sweeps the floorboards. I think about how well she looked after Dad and me.

The calendar on the wall shifts in the wind. Mum has turned the room into a sewing room. The calendar is only one month behind. Mum, old-fashioned as she is, has put in dates, like people's birthdays. I'm surprised that there are some dates from my dad's side of the family. When I was growing up, here in this bedroom, the sound of the cars on the highway sounded like the ocean. I know the ocean now. I know Ki. I take a breath in, shut my eyes. I do want to stop what they're doing to Ki. Any loyalty I had to Milligan or the corporation has long ceased. From the beginning I'd known there was something more, and now I know the truth.

My mobile phone is out of battery so I don't know if Milligan tried to call me when I didn't show up this morning to pick up the formula from Jack. How long until they cancel my security pass, break into my housing, put my name and photo on high alert? During my time there, I haven't exactly stayed under the radar, perhaps like Uncle and Julie might have wanted me to for their plan to work. Maybe I've already been labelled a radicalist, being AWOL today, particularly with my family background. Any longer and they might figure it out. All of it.

Sometime during the day I step out of the dark like a white-capped mushroom, to make a phone call.

My mum looks at me in surprise when I come out. We sit down at the kitchen table. 'Julie called. A lot of times. I told her you were asleep.'

'Thanks.'

'Should I have not told her you're here?' Her brow is wrinkled.

'No.' I touch her hand with my own.

'I'm worried about you,' she says.

I ask to use her phone. Julie answers on the first ring.

Her voice is strained, 'Kaden, cuz, I'm ...'

'I'm in,' I say.

Julie picks me up an hour later. Mum also comes with us. Our mob is gathering on the foreshore at the Cleveland esplanade for a barbecue. A good feed, with good company. My family, many of whom I haven't seen for years, like my Uncle Theo and his seven children, my cousins. Some of them have their own children. I look over at my mum, who is reuniting with Uncle Theo's wife, Sunny. There are more families: Aboriginal, Islander and non-Indigenous. Hugh and his family are there.

I eat fried fish and salad. The islands are blue shapes in the distance. The group is performing a ceremony by the water. I sit by myself.

Julie comes over to me. 'Are you okay?'

I nod. 'I'm a little better. It's just ... Julie ... how can we sacrifice ... Have you met them? Hinter ... and Larapinta?'

She nods in understanding. 'They want this, too.'

'Larapinta reads,' I say.

She touches my shoulder. 'This is for them.' She points at the ceremony by the water. I look at Uncle Ron and the others. I see that they are holding petals of native orchids. They are dropping them into the sea.

After this and when everyone is fed, Uncle Ron talks about the approach and strategies again. It will happen tomorrow. I know what I have to do.

When Julie drops me off at the ferry terminal, guilt flashes across her face. 'I bet you're wishing you never got back in touch with me.'

I shake my head.

She continues with a sideways glance at my mother, 'You don't have to do this. You can go back to your life.'

'How can I go back? How can I unknow what I know now? I've been in the dark for far too long. I know who I am now. I know what we have to do.'

She hugs me. My mother also hugs me goodbye. Both of them wait and wave me off.

I find Larapinta at the hidden slice of the beach, by the rotting jetty. Her roots shoot out when she sees me, her face shows some glint and when I reach out to her she entwines our fingers together.

I tell her I know what they are. They're my old people. They're spirits of thousands of years.

'So if you're back, it means you are with us,' she says.

'Yes, tomorrow.' A shake starts in my knees and she comforts me until it stops. She walks me home and I lean on her. She tells me she kept the secret to protect me. She doesn't know how they, as jangigir, came to be in the form they are in, but they know their purpose.

The house already smells musky and feels strange after my long day away from it. I turn on the lamp on the bedside table.

'Let me make you something to eat,' Larapinta says.

'I don't need ...'

'Yes, you do. Sit down.'

I hear the sounds of her roots tapping against the kitchen tiles, her flowered fingers opening drawers, fixing the cutting board. When I open my eyes I see she has made me an artichoke sandwich.

'Thank you,' I say.

'You are too tired.'

I eat sitting across from her. It is almost impossible to get food down.

'Why don't you run away with me?' I say. But I know it's damn near foolish. Now, without me, without her, without us, there is no ancestral country, there is no Ki, there is no Moreton Bay.

But we have rooted, here, in this room, because anything outside means loss, and losing one another is like the cutting of history, the shredding of encyclopaedias.

I wait for her to say something, something that will be so very unhuman and unemotional. And she does, she talks logically about the weather: which way the wind will blow tomorrow to get them on course. I tell her to turn around and look at the window as I take off my clothes. The blinds are open and there is only darkness outside. I see her pale reflection in the window, and I see my own breasts as I pull off my tank top. We make eye contact as I step out of my jeans.

The kiss is like a crash. Without her hand – supporting my head, my neck, my shoulders – I would have whiplash. She puts her mouth in the flat between my breasts. Rubs her cheek against my nipple. I feel like all I can hear in my head is a speedboat travelling through water.

The sheets are cold when we find ourselves on the bed. She does not say one word and her eyes are like glow moths attracted to the light.

'I'm not human,' Larapinta reminds me. 'You never used to let me forget it.'

In the early hours of the morning, when I walk out of the house I have been living in these past few weeks, and shine the torch across the street, I see that the trees have started to shed their leaves, and the yellow flowers stick to my feet as I walk by. I stop outside the house with the pick-up truck and walk over to the passenger's side. A few hours earlier I had dropped in and asked if I could borrow the truck, and my neighbour had given me the keys. Now I start it up and head for the coloured buildings, the Science Centre. I've eaten my last custard tart, and it wasn't perfect. It was a bit too eggy and the pastry had crumbled in my bag.

Larapinta left last night to gather the jangigir. She told me I had been very helpful in not giving the jangigir the formula for a week, as it had been designed to make them weak and docile. By today they will be at full strength. Larapinta has left me her e-reader, and she took no weapon. I know she has abilities and qualities that are not yet known to me, and I naively hope these would be enough so that we might see each other again.

I get out of the vehicle casually. If anyone's here, if anyone questions me, I'm a little early for work this morning because I missed yesterday. It's quiet. I shine my way to the door. My heart flutters when I wave my security pass at the signal. To my relief it flashes green and unlocks. I twist the handle. It is dark inside and I don't bother turning on the lights. I get on a computer and log in – then do what Julie has told me. Her computer code gets through the security walls and into the camera system and shuts it all down. Julie said it will act as a temporary glitch and last an hour. They have these glitches all the time, so it won't be too suspicious. I set the stopwatch on my phone.

The security on all the doors has also temporarily lifted. I walk quickly into the lab and get the new formula they have been developing. The one that will kill the jangigir. I carry all the formula out using a trolley I found in the bays. I go out the doors and load the formula onto the truck. It will go straight into the sea and dilute harmlessly.

I think our resistance has a chance. The plan was moulded around defence and attack. My part is to disable their systems, and take the weapons they would use against us, including the research and the recipe for the formula. Larapinta and my uncle have developed a plan to lay siege to Ki Island and abolish the infrastructure, using the combined forces of men and jangigir. I hope we have the numbers.

I drive the few extra hundred metres to the building next to the Science Centre, the orange one, which was the hospital and security base. I know that I can't expect there won't be people here and I'm worried about finding company. I have dressed like a security guard, white shirt, black pants. My hair's tied back under a hat. Hopefully, they won't look closely enough at my badges. I swipe myself in and keep my head down as I walk down the hallway. I pass a few people working with their backs to me. I have memorised the building's layout from the map one of my uncle's friends has given me. I sneak down the next hallway and into the storage facility opposite the medical supply room where they keep the weapons. I get in the room, take out my torch, and obtain three pistols and a weight of ammunition. I put it all in my bag, the company one they gave me when I started. There are five other pistols, more than I thought, and I remove the firing pins the way my uncle has showed me, pocket them, and place the guns back. Then I walk the hell out of there.

The bag is already getting heavy. Sweat is dripping from the hair pressed under my hat onto my face and into my ears. It is a miracle that I run into no one before I reach the door. In the car park I get into the vehicle, lying the bag down on the passenger's seat, and hit the engine. As I shoulder out I see in the rear-view mirror a worker come out and look at me.

When I get to the ferry terminal the boat is already there, a worn ferry that my uncle has got his hands on. It has been painted with one of my father's designs and his signature is lopsided on the cabin. I know it moves twice as fast as the old tinny. My relatives, mostly burly dark men with biceps I'm jealous of, quickly come up and offer to help transfer the formula. They take the guns with a sense of urgency.

My uncle stands in the prow holding onto the bowrail, his grey-white beard swinging in the breeze. He seems to be waiting for me to come to him.

I have promised Julie and my mother that this is the last of my involvement. That I will sit down here on the metal chairs and wait for the next ferry to the mainland, due in seventeen minutes. In that time, even from here, I will hear the sound of the jangigir overcoming the guards on Ki and ripping up the underwater wires and machinery. They will form a circle protecting Ki Island. And the people aboard the ferry will enter that threshold, holding the guns, just in case. I want to be alongside them. I look at my stopwatch again. More than half an hour has passed. I walk closer to the ferry and call to my uncle. Then see a movement out of the corner of my eye.

In the clear water behind the ferry I can see them. They are everywhere. Stretching out as far as my vision reaches. And then I know there are as many behind them. The brown reeds of their hair are all that is showing. They move in formations, in shapes similar to the last letter of the alphabet. Larapinta is one of them. There must be thousands. I step onto the ferry and stand next to my uncle. The water is rising around us and I can feel the force in the leaping waves and what we're about to do.

LIGHT

Strike Another Match

The blackfella fashion here is contagious. Kitty wears a flanno over a blackfella T-shirt with a long floral red skirt and Dunlop volleys. I ain't looking too flash like them mob here, even the little fellas with their basketball caps and mismatched sneakers. My glamour does not translate in desert country, red stains down the seams of my white pants. I need a hat to replace this crowding sun. The memory intrudes of the summer I spent with one married woman, a redhead, name buried because she is famous, or she lives her life with famous people and she is only famous by default. She rubbed sunscreen down the insides of my arms. I know you don't burn, honey, she said. But I want to see you protected. Now, I think she did have a slight American accent, but I didn't notice it often. I remember asking her if she was born in my city, and she answered perplexed. I'm from Dallas, honey. She left marks on me despite my gritted teeth because I had fallen for as many women that year as I had stopped for fuel and it was proving costly. They all tried to denounce their relationship status as little more than an old faded tattoo easily covered, but married was not what I was looking for. Tell you what,

I still don't know what it is I'm looking for but Alice is a good enough place to start. I feel like walking in a straight line through the desert with a metal detector pointed to the ground.

Real Moment

When I was growing up in Hervey Bay, the closest I got to a Real Gay Moment was when Maria Hapeta put a kiss on the Christmas card she gave to me.

High school was counter-intuitive to me. All I wanted was to fish and swim on my grandmother's country in the best hours of the day. But I had to go to classes and mix with white kids, and think about 'what I wanted to do'. So many decisions. I had gone to a Murri primary school. Now at high school I was the only black girl in my grade, though some kids were Maori, like Maria. People asked me why I didn't hang out with the Toby boys. I told them it was because they thought killing frogs was cool.

I didn't find out 'what I wanted to do' until I was fifteen. School was keeping me up at night. I was often awake in the flat hours of the morning, trying to 'find myself', or what-ever, by eating cheese rings and playing Justin Timberlake just loud enough in the living room. On one of these evenings I turned on the TV and, surprisingly, SBS was working – our television was notoriously two-channel, which was why I never brought any of the white kids home after school. It was a French film, black-and-white, about two actresses living poor in Paris, trying to get a break. Don't bother looking for it, I've searched many times over the years. One of the main characters was honey blond and the other was brunette. The brunette was a lesbian, I know this because they walked into a pub and one of the men pointed at her and yelled and the subtitle came up with the word 'dyke'. I tried to look it up in the dictionary, but I knew what the word meant. For some reason, the video recorder had been left on, by my brother maybe, and it filmed the movie almost entirely. That whole week, I would re-watch the film in the early hours, convince myself I wanted to be an actress, like the brunette. I watched the scene in the bar closely: the brunette walking in with her motorcycle boots and opening her jacket, her lips pursed as she looked at another woman standing in the corner, the way she turned her head to the man as he said that word and drew her eyes down as if she had been slapped.

I moved to Sydney after high school, getting into the second-tier acting college. Mum and Dad had come around to it by then, and anyway, there isn't much you can do to stop a hell-bent eighteen-year-old. I enjoyed my study in a dull sort of way, but I really enjoyed Sydney more than anything else, the clear harbour, the quiet old streets in The Rocks and the fast-moving people always around me. I was walking there one time in the afternoon and I literally stopped at the sight of two short-haired women stepping out of a cafe holding hands across the road. The taller one turned to the other woman and brushed her hair to the side, and then they both leant in for a kiss that was obstructed by the sudden traffic spilling down the lane. In a second they were gone; I wasn't even sure if they had gone in the direction of the city or harbour. All I knew was that I was shaking, and had come to the realisation that this was part of the reason I had come here.

The next few weeks I tried to leapfrog myself into the unknown. I stood outside the clubs on Oxford Street, and was rejected entry because my only form of ID was a student card. I went to the bookshop, which was still open (I couldn't comprehend a bookshop being open at 10 p.m. – in Hervey Bay, bookshops didn't exist). I was overwhelmed by the gay titles everywhere. I made my way to the lesbian section and scoured the shelves, my attention caught by butch and fem cowgirl erotica and *101 Lesbian Sex Positions*. I timidly opened one up, my mind exploding at the stories spilling from the page.

I glanced at the register. The girl was tattooed with wide-rimmed glasses. She gazed back at me. I looked down at the book again, my breathing heavy. There was no way I could leave the store with this book, or any on that shelf. I walked out, red to the neck, passing a group of well-dressed arty types. I wouldn't go to Oxford Street again. Instead, I began to breakfast at one of the sidewalk cafes in The Rocks, even though I could only afford the croissant with a coffee, in the hope that I would see those women again, or girls like them.

At college things were more than fine. I had made friends with quite a few Koori students, Jai and Annie in particular. Jai was from Newcastle and had been a good water-polo player until he quit for dancing. He was quick with his humour, having a one-liner for everything you might say to him. Annie was quieter, like me. She was a

Wik woman, who sometimes cooked traditional food when she invited us to her flat. The best thing that happened was that Jai decided he needed a new computer, so he gave me his old one for a folded fifty-dollar note and a few drinks at the social society. It was my first computer, and I spent a wealth of time on it. I started with a Google search of lesbian erotica. After hours, I would lie back on the bed with my hand underneath me.

Even though I had good friends, I was lonely in my closeted, un-acted-upon existence. This settled a little bit when I found out Jai was bisexual. I would go with him to his performances on a Friday night at the theatre, and it would be crawling with young queer boys. I would sit there by the outdoor stage and watch Jai talk to them. He was such an easy talker, he never showed fear of the unknown. I was there every Friday night, although as far as I could tell, the only queer attendees were male. I was very hopeful, the way I scoured the crowd every week, just as ambitious as my regular attendance at that cafe in the Rocks.

Whenever I went home for a week and saw Mum and Dad and my older brother, I'd be hit by a surge of homesickness to think that I would have to go back to campus. On the first night, Dad would make his mean fish stew, and after eating we would go for a walk along the beach. Most of all, it was never cold. My legs browned, though I only wore jeans in Sydney anyway. Even though I loved to be home, I felt distanced from my parents a little bit, uncomfortable even. Mum didn't ask if I'd 'met a boy down there', but her friends did. I considered telling my brother I thought I was queer. It was funny because I'd always expected he would be the gay one. In primary school he dressed up in my ballet outfits and developed boy crushes on action movie heroes. He played homo-erotic pranks on his mates in the football team. Now he was engaged to a very nice Samoan woman who worked for Queensland Rail and got our family free travel. I didn't feel like I could tell him – only five years ago it seemed like none of this would happen. I was so happy for him but I felt an impending nervousness about going to their wedding. All my Aunties would be like, 'It's your turn next, bub.' I did want my turn at love, but not in the way anyone in my family would expect.

In a grade eleven drama assignment, I had been grouped with Maria Hapeta. I had liked her since grade seven, though we had drifted in and out of each other's social circles by then. When she called me over to be part of the group, she gave me a wide smile and I blushed. We developed a script as a modern response to *Romeo and Juliet*, and because there were only girls in our group, I was elected Romeo. This always happened to me. Must have been my arms and my height and how I took out the whole swimming carnival every year. It started way back in primary school when I was made Sporty Spice instead of my preference, Baby. Maria was an obvious Juliet. Her skin was shiny like cellophane paper and her teeth were like shells. I was nervously anticipating this one scene we wrote in, where Romeo rolls up to Juliet at a petrol station in a beat-up Corolla and tells her she's pretty hot. Then Romeo, or me, kisses Juliet, or Marie, before being busted by Juliet's father who threatens to fix him up.

We had done this peck thing in rehearsals, though I assumed we would go for it fully in the presentation for the class. Working with Maria got my blood jumping. She was so sweet to me, and she didn't have to be. When the day came I ironed my shirt and slipped breath mints in my bag. But Maria would not kiss me. She did an elaborate neck trick so it looked like we were lip-locked, but no contact was made. Even though none of my classmates mentioned it, I felt so shame afterwards, so much so that I contemplated quitting drama.

Jai, Annie and I started a mentoring program for the younger Aboriginal students that came through the arts and performance school. In general, I was surprised about how switched-on and confident these first-years were from the get-go. Most of them had grown up in Sydney and wore flash jackets and dresses and stuff. I had come down from Hervey Bay with one pair of Target jeans and a handful of paint-splattered T-shirts.

My lecturers were really pushing me to do my best. With such a small group, some of the projects were quite emotional. I did a lot of performance pieces about being Murri. When I was up there on stage, I sometimes looked into the crowd, which often just filled the first two rows, and I wondered if there was someone out there for me.

In the end, after three years, it was in a grocery store that I met her. I had finished my degree and it was my last shop before I left for home on the weekend. My mum and dad were ecstatic about me coming back. Annie had got a gig lined up straightaway and Jai was staying on, but I had worked out I would go back to Hervey Bay and try to find some kind of work there, at least for the time being.

She was different from most of the people in the store, as she wore workers clothes and her red hair was up. We passed each other a few times in the aisles. I tried not to look at her, as I did with most straight-looking women I found attractive. I had this feeling that they would *know*, by my look, and be disgusted. She came up next to me while I was choosing mints for the plane trip.

'Excuse me,' she said. 'Where's the soup?'

'I don't know,' I said quickly. 'Why don't you ask … ?' I looked for a shop attendant.

'There's no one around.' She smiled. 'Short-staffed.'

'Must be because of the end of uni,' I said.

'Are you a student?' She looked so sophisticated. Red lipstick.

'Ah, no.' I cleared my throat. 'I think I know where the soup is.'

'I'll follow you,' she said. 'It must seem funny, buying soup in summer.'

'Hadn't thought of it even.'

She continued. 'We're having a fire to celebrate the end of semester. It's hard to think what to put on the fire. Soup works, I think.'

'Oh,' I said. 'You're a student.'

'Finished now.' She was balancing two zucchinis and a bag of lollies in her hand.

I hadn't seen her around, but us arts mob more or less were quarantined from the rest of the student body. She followed me down aisle five, the pasta aisle, which looked promising.

She was saying, 'I got a job just at the finish, though. Real estate.'

'You like it?' I asked.

'No,' she said. 'I wish I spent more time on exams instead. Ah, here it is!' She grabbed a tin off the shelf, smiling, suddenly excited. 'Thank you! You're welcome to come tonight.'

'No worries,' I said.

'We're in Bell Lane, babe.'

It so happened that Annie was going to the same party, which I realised when I met her for coffee, so she said she would pick me up. I wore new navy chinos, a white shirt and sneakers. We stopped at the bottle-o on campus and arrived at eight. There were so many people there. I saw the girl from the supermarket, whom Annie knew and introduced as Sally. She knew Sally from tennis. I looked at Sally's calves, and I knew she would play quite well. She was wearing more casual clothes than this afternoon, short jean shorts and a tank top. The music was good, a bit of reggae. I noticed immediately that Sally had a lot of dykey friends. When I chatted to them I realised Sally had a girl-friend, a skinny, boyish girl wearing a stripy shirt.

One of the dykes was African, and her eyes lingered on me, making me nervous. She was very cool. At ten-ish a lot of people left for another party, including Annie, and Sally's girlfriend. I had drunk too much and finally went to the bathroom, which was down the hallway. The African girl was washing her hands. We were almost trapped in the tiny sharehouse bathroom, wall to wall. She looked up at me and I mumbled something about coming back, leaving.

On the deck again I lay down in the hammock and soon Sally came and sat next to me. We talked about living away from family, tennis, and the power of the night. I told her it was my last in Sydney and she said she hoped it would be one I'd remember. Her body so close was making me dizzy.

I asked about her girlfriend, I'd forgotten her name, and why she hadn't stayed.

'Who said she's my girlfriend?' Sally replied, and she stared into my eyes until I pulled away and she smirked a little.

I barely noticed when she left for brief moments – to say goodbye to friends or get another beer out of the fridge or do something else related to being a host of a party. I only noticed when I realised we were the only ones left, and my watch said 2.30 a.m. She smiled warmly, her breasts pulled towards me, though contained in the singlet.

'You got anywhere to be?' she asked me.

'Not really.'

'My roommates have left for tonight. I should clean up, but I think I'll wait until they come back in the morning. It was mostly their friends that made the mess, anyway. Girls are a lot tidier.'

'Yeah,' I said.

'Would you like to go into my room? It's cooler.'

I wasn't warm, but I didn't tell her that.

We went in and lay side by side on the double bed. She kicked off her thongs and pulled off her shirt, revealing a pink bra. I didn't know what was happening. Then she leant over and started kissing me and telling me to take my clothes off – and in a rush we were naked and I was trying to breathe. It was what I had wanted for so long and I could hardly believe it, I kept thinking about her asking me about soup, and realised I hadn't eaten a thing that night.

I looked at her in the pinch of the light. Her body was a perfect balance of soft and hard, of lean and curve.

'Are you okay?' she asked at one point.

'Yeah,' I stammered. 'Just quiet.'

'Well, that's good, as I don't want to talk,' she said, and she brought my fingers to her slick opening and I gasped at the need of her. She was quick to come and she brought her still-shuddering body on to mine and rocked her pubic bone hard into me. I felt so warm my skin burned. I gripped her soft buttocks closer to me until I let out a sharp cry, followed by another. She rolled off me, we held hands and she fell asleep.

I reached for my clothes in the darkness to go to the bathroom. I had lost all sense of anything outside the room, her roommates may have come back, the days may have changed. I put on my underwear and my chinos at once, and tenderly reached for her tank top on the floor and pulled it over my breasts.

I went into the bathroom, turned on the light, and shut the door behind me. I sat on the toilet seat and looked down between my legs, amazed at the glistening wet mark on my underwear, like glitter. With toilet paper I explored the extent of my wetness. My legs were still shaking. I saw the tag inside my pants. *This colour will continue to fade*, it said.

Anything Can Happen

A few weeks after Lucy moved in she said we needed a new broom. I was on my laptop, probably looking up sneakers on eBay, and I didn't pay much attention. The next few times she mentioned it I don't think I bothered even looking at the broom. To me, it was a faceless constant. I knew my mother had given me the broom and I knew there wasn't anything wrong with it.

For months Lucy made sure the broom was on shopping lists and waiting-for-the-bus conversation. Though she was all talk, no action.

'Why don't you just get one?' I said when I was fed up.

'I don't want to carry it home,' she said.

I imagined her tiny frame carrying it over her shoulder. Neither of us had cars then. I knew she was looking at me and my boxing arms still sweaty from the gym. She was butching me up, just as I femmed her up if I felt like a chip sandwich when I got home from work late or when her sister was coming over and the toilet hadn't been cleaned.

Lucy knew my mum had gone. It was in October, Mum had just got laid off at the post office and I had taken her out to plane-spot from Toona Lane. It was also my twentieth birthday so it was probably more of a thing I chose for myself. We sat there in the car and the planes shuddered any space we thought we had from the sky. Poor Mum. It had been the only job she'd ever liked and they hadn't called her Denise.

We got out of the car. What happened in those next few minutes is that Mum moved before I could notice and I didn't start chasing her straightaway because I had no shoes on, and I didn't know she was going to do what she did.

In short, she got over the fence and onto the runway; she stood there wearing her Aboriginal flag T-shirt, there was a small Qantas plane, coasting, and they stopped to let her on.

Without an explanation or a backward look at me, my mother surged forward into the space and was collected. All preparations were completed, the plane gained speed, then height, and soon it was tiny in the distance, looking like an asterisk on a page.

I tracked the plane and found out it was the weekly flight to Port Hedland. I bet she's happy there and she has got a new job already. She doesn't send postcards but I get a throaty voicemail every now and then.

But that's not what really happened, Lucy says – and what can I say, doesn't she think I've gone over it a thousand times in my head, but that's what I remember.

Lucy asks so many questions I can't answer that I don't bother talking about it anymore, it's easier that way.

After Christmas we finally saved up for a second-hand Suzuki Swift and I'm driving us to Bunnings to get some plants because we're all 'settled' and shit, when Lucy mentions it would be nice to get the broom while we're here.

We go down a few of those long aisles. It's not with the 'garden tools'. There's just spades and rakes.

'Of course,' I say out loud. 'These are for outside use. They don't sell brooms here, Lucy.'

'I would use it for outside as well.' Lucy sniffs. 'To sweep up those little yellow flowers that always spread across the concrete like confetti.'

'Why don't you ask someone, then?'

'Why don't you?'

'I need a drink,' I say. 'It's the driving.'

I leave her by the fertiliser and go to the cafe and get a flavoured water from the fridge. The woman doesn't look up from making coffees even though I know she's seen me. I'm sure I'm not the only homemaking lesbian she's seen today, though she doesn't serve me until after a man and his two kids come over.

I find Lucy in the outdoor section wrestling a peace lily.

'Where have you been? I needed your help.'

'Getting my drink, where do you think? I wasn't just twirling my thumbs.'

'Twiddling,' she says. 'I don't want to spend all day here.'

We end up having a full-on couple's fight and draw a crowd. Obviously something deeper is driving Lucy to behave like this for a broom, though I of course have my own hang-ups about it.

It is me who surrenders. I take Lucy to our next

Sunday-shop stop, Woolworths, and buy her a spanking-new sixteen-dollar broom.

I push it into the back seat of the car and I feel that twinge of remorse when it fits sideways and I can shut the door.

When we get home, Lucy spends so much time sweeping our floorboards she's late for work. After she leaves I feel alone, but I also feel alive.

I find myself missing a lot of things about my mother. Like how she would come over with a twenty-four-pack of toilet paper when it was on special at Aldi. She sewed the same holes in my favourite jeans. She would ring me up at work when she saw a storm on the radar and warn me about leaving. She brought over her neighbour's lemons when I called her up with a cold. She liked to make Lucy and me stuff, especially clothes. She knitted Lucy three scarves the month we first started dating. Lucy says she could have got out then.

Lucy only got to meet Mum a couple of times. The first time we went over there, Mum had the TV on one of those bride-themed reality shows. Lucy made a face while we sat there. I told her I'd show her downstairs and the yard. She brushed her lips to my ear as we walked down the stairs and said, 'I just can't stand not touching you.' We ended up getting it on in the laundry and in our disorientated state did not hear Mum come down. We hadn't turned the light on, and we stood there, wrapped into each other, as Mum, not seeing us, moved to within metres and put the washing basket down next to the machine. We watched Mum fill the machine, unable to move or we'd give ourselves away. We heard Mum whispering to herself, 'Oh, no, Delise, why did you have to say that?' Also, 'She sure is pretty, almost too pretty,' and, 'Do I ask them who's the man, who's the woman?'

My mother turns up everywhere now. In the pop-up ads on my browser and on late night talkback radio. I know there are people I look unconsciously at for motherly figures. Possible candidates include: my Taekwondo instructor, my doting but vague colleague, my long-lost Aunty and the middle-aged checkout chick.

That night Lucy comes home at her usual time and I am used to her routine of cleaning up all over again as if it was somehow forgotten in the hours she was gone. Through the darkness I look down to see that the neighbours have left their washing on the line. We watch the basketball on the Olympics and drink Japanese beer. I am amused by the pole vault and Lucy is in awe of the gymnastics. I put my face into Lucy's beer-smelling hair and we go upstairs and sleep.

We both know how important time together is. I work days and she works nights. Lucy and I didn't have a spectacular beginning, but we don't mind. We were friends and now we are partners. There wasn't really a moment I could say we got together. I just know we started sitting close on the bus to town and sleeping at each other's places. She is my first girlfriend and I am hers and I don't think about last because that's too much right now but she knows she has my heart – and at the moment that only equates to how we coloured in each other's Cons with our shapes and initials.

In the morning I lay fresh eyes on the broom Mum got me, and with these fresh eyes I've come around to the fact that it is kind of broken and it needs to go. There is not enough room in our flat for sentimentality, that's what I used to say. To Mum actually. I didn't enjoy her gifts when I got them. I give the broom a proper funeral and choose a numbered bin outside our complex for it to rest in until tomorrow morning when the collectors come.

I have a memory chain of Mum that I can only recall through photographs. I was five and it was summer and Dad was never around. Mum walked me around the block every morning and we spent time in the playground. We went to the milk bar to pick up groceries and when she had some spare money she would get me a fresh apple juice. We went everywhere together. We wore matching headbands. She made me a crocodile costume for my birthday. We went on a trip to the mountains and I was scared of the cows on the way. The tooth fairy came in the night. Then I started grade one at the school down the road. We cried together. She said she'd be there waiting at three, even earlier. She always was.

She read to me every night so I wasn't lonely in my dreams. It wasn't usually from books, but stories she created. Not about princesses and dragons and magic carpets. About the cheeky gecko named Larry that came to our bathroom window and the emu that could fly.

Lucy is very pedantic when it comes to our place. She notices when I mess with the fridge magnets, even just a little bit. She won't allow shoes in the house and when I come home from gym I can't sit on the couch, or even just lurk around, until I'm showered. Lucy delights in a perfectly kept home and garden.

Lucy really shits me when she DJs our car and bus trips. There is no sense of the unknown about it, every song is measured. At the traffic lights I try to talk to her about my family but she's not listening.

My dad was eaten by a tiger. He had just started on a new dose of medication for his heart condition. He was camping with a friend at the time and they said when my dad saw the tiger he just started charging at it. The tiger had dropped from a tree right in front of them. This tiger had developed an appetite for humans. It was a long struggle between the tiger and Dad. Post mortem he had bites to his thigh, chest, throat and face. They found some of the possessions Dad had on him. He had a photo of me in his wallet.

I remembered my mother, Lucy and me sitting around the dinner table.

'So, Lucy, what do you do?' my mum said, piling more greens on my plate. She had a habit of not allowing herself to eat until everyone had finished.

'I work at the entertainment centre,' she said. 'I collect people's tickets.'

'Uh-huh,' Mum said. 'And are you studying?'

'No.'

Mum started unloading the dishwasher.

I said, 'Lucy studied teaching. Early childhood.'

'And do you have any plans to get into teaching?'

'I didn't finish,' Lucy said pointedly.

They talked about me. The big news was that I was getting my wisdom teeth out on the coming Friday.

'I'll pick you up at eight,' Mum said.

'Thanks—' I started.

'That's okay,' Lucy said. 'I've already arranged to take her there, and I've taken the night off work, too.'

My mum looked at Lucy with a surprised expression. 'You don't have a car. And she was going to stay the night here.'

'It's okay, Luce,' I quickly said. 'You can come in the car with us.'

'I don't know,' Mum said. 'I was going to get my hair done at the Gabba while I was waiting for you.'

Lucy's normally sweet face looked then like a run-over pie. I remembered Mum had made the same face when she commented on my new laptop bag and I said Lucy had made it for me for my birthday. They were both fighting not to be obsolete.

I flip open my laptop to check the time in Port Hedland. It is 10 a.m. and I bet Mum's on the beach, shades on so no one knows she's thinking of a daughter left behind. I go out to the street and open the lid of the third bin. I push up on the edge and the bin holds my weight as I do a sort of improvised exercise, all the while looking down into the dark throat of the bin at the handle of the broom. It isn't long until Lucy comes and asks me what I'm doing.

Lungs

In order, this is where I feel it. Hands, feet, lips, tits. The sun's left and it's gone cold on me. I walk back into the store, up the aisles and to the dry space we've blocked off at the side, in the deli section. Mark's spread all the towels and items from the clothing section on the floor. I pick up a hoodie and put it around my shoulders. It's slightly damp and smells like prawns.

'Cold?' Mark laughs at me. 'It's fucking January. It's fucking Rockhampton.'

I sit down with my back against the wall.

Mark comes up beside me. 'It's the wet clothes. You should change.'

'You put 'em all on the floor.'

'Nah, not all of it. Go see for yourself. Underwear and socks and some other things.' He looks at me. 'Look, I know we're probably both going to start getting cold. But I'm thinking we should light a fire, they'll see us then, too.'

I notice he's still wearing his name badge.

'How we going to do that?'

'You would know, wouldn't you?' Mark says. He rubs his hands together, cups them to his face, makes didgeridoo sounds.

I look away from him and get up. 'I'm going to go look in the car park again. See if I can get into one of those cars.'

'We've already tried that like a hundred times.'

'Yeah, well.' I want to say it's better than sitting here with him next to the cheese.

We have had nothing in common before this day apart from being the only oldies working at the checkouts – well, old compared to the rest of the lot, fifteen-year-old high-school kids. Management usually put one of us at the cigarette counter, as we're supposed to be responsible.

A few moments later the lights go out. We swear and reach in our pockets for our torches. When they turn on we both catch each other looking shocking against the white walls.

'I'll go down,' I say, my intention in the first place. 'There must be a second switch.'

Mark holds his hands up in the air. 'This will be interesting,' he smirks.

Before I step out I put on the hoodie properly. I kick through the water swirling around the supermarket floor. I get outside, where the water is at knee-height. The water rises as I step down the ramp. At least it's warm water. It doesn't feel too good against my hands, though. My skin and Mark's skin are peeling. We've already gone through one bottle of moisturiser.

When I'm down in the car park, something brushes against my leg and I'm unsure if I imagined it or not. I resist the temptation to squeal. I don't want Mark coming down here and thinking I can't do the job.

I see the generator and turn it on, and it's a relief when the light floods from above. It's then that I see it, the thing in the water. It's some sort of fish or eel. It's bobbing along in the water, head in the shallows, its eyes just under. It does a few circles, the tail gliding it through the water. Its movements are weak. I need to get it out.

'Oi!' Now that the lights are on, of course Mark has come down to check on me. I see his torso, his green shirt coming down the ramp.

He's in his usual form. 'What are you doing with that?' is his first reaction. Next is: 'If you're going to get it out of there, we may as well eat it.'

'I'm getting it out,' I reply, nodding. I pick it up and it holds steady in my arms. I wade through the water.

Mark steps in front of me. 'No no, you're an idiot. Is this like what happened with the Lancer? Oh, fuck me.'

Yesterday, when my clothes were still half-dry, we were out of the store, the storm had just passed and we were checking out the damage to the roof. Things were going past us pretty quickly. Anything from wood to signposts to fridges. I saw the sailing red Lancer, a few metres out, moving steadily. It looked empty, but then, in the back window, a small face came up, hands pressed against the glass. A young boy, maybe six. I yelled and I went in the water, chest down, but Mark got me by the hair and I struggled long enough to watch the car go.

Mark's still talking to me. 'You got to stop this. No more of it.'

★

I find some heat in a high cupboard, usually stocked with bread. It was one of the items that went first, when they announced the possible flood, the evacuation. I wonder if people outside the store are still eating the bread, or whether it's gone off already. I curl up in the shelf and nurse the space between my arms in which I carried the lungfish out of the car park.

There was a picture of it in one of the magazines, I remember. We'd made a stack of the mags up high in the office. I hadn't read them yet. I wasn't ready to commit to weight loss and crosswords and Sudoku. In this *National Geographic* magazine, it had a picture of the lungfish and its name. The lungfish I held had those tiny pin-like eyes. An expressive face, for a fish. While we moved, I felt the rough cuts underneath its belly. I encouraged the lift of it and it wobbled out of my grip. I saw its tail leap over the white traffic pickets. I think it made it but I can't be sure.

I had a kid when I was fifteen and I dropped out of school. I was kind of blacked-out then. I gave birth to a baby boy, and I named him Samuel. He was so tiny and he died at two weeks old from complications to his heart. They said complications to his heart but I just thought about how I never really wanted him in the first place and that's what really killed him. I was too young then. I didn't know what to do. I have been working at this supermarket for a long time now and I keep an eye on the fifteen-year-old girls. I wait for them to make the same mistakes that I did. But none of them do.

The boy I saw in the Lancer was real, I know, not just a figure of a never-really-was mother's imagination. In our base spot in the deli section, I hear Mark is playing around with the radio, trying to get a station. I listen through the crackle for a mention of the red Lancer. I think of leaving Mark, to search for the boy inside the car. The lungfish will come with me, too. It will grow into a dolphin-like thing, and I'll travel on it over the river this flood has made.

Mark comes down the aisle. 'Look what I've got! Condoms!' He tosses me a packet that I don't reach for. It hits the water and floats. 'Not that we're going to need them if we're going to repopulate the planet.'

I finally tell him to fuck off.

I get up from the shelf, put my hands in my pockets and shuffle around the store.

The water is receding and soon they will find us. I'm not sure if the lungfish will matter then: other people's and community's battle stories, the contagion of trauma, will outdo it. I feel it in my chest.

Paddles, Not Oars

Kela sat up cross-legged in his bed as his mother slept. He took his sock off to squish a cockie against the wall. He put his hand out the window, riding the cold air, and checked the flag was still positioned well.

For his thirteenth birthday his mother had got him a bag of marshmallows and a second-hand encyclopaedia set, A to E. That month he got a weekend job on the construction site, a block away from their flat, for the new overpass.

One afternoon he headed down by the pier and used marshmallows as bait, thought he'd bring home some dinner. He rubbed the dried mud off his cheek as he waited. His father had taught him to read the stars. Hours must've passed because his mother screamed at him from the beach. Flat from walking the blocks, still in her cannery outfit. 'From now on I'll get Fran to pick you up.'

A couple of weeks went by before they got the knock on the door saying they were tearing down the building, and they had three weeks to find another place. Three weeks came and Kela's mother packed up the car and they got on the highway. Kela tried to talk to his mother. He watched her grip on the steering wheel.

'We're going to your aunt's,' his mother said. Kela's body clenched the souther they got. He could already feel his legs growing cold in his boardshorts.

With nothing left to do, he read from the encyclopaedia until it grew dark outside. They stopped at Coffs that night. His mother parked next to the caravan park by the water. Kela watched the waves skate in. He thought about his father. He saw the canoe in the sky. His mother sat in the back next to him, a blanket over both of them. She told him stories of his father, talking herself to sleep. She'd always sleep before him, and he played his usual night games with himself, counting numbers, remembering the encyclopaedia entries: *albino*, *Banda Banda volcano*, *CIA* and repeating things his father had told him. There were so many stories that his father had never got to finish. And here the sky was different.

He had gotten through the organisational structure of the CIA when the lights of a vehicle approached. He crawled over the seats and parked himself in the front, pulling his mother's pillow out from under him, he didn't need it. He turned the ignition. His father wanted to teach him on his grandmother's property. When Mum's not around, he had said. She was always around.

The wheel felt heavier than he expected. He reversed back onto the road and drove in the opposite direction to the car, which was pulling in. The car would be coppas or the men involved with his father. They were going after him now. He pulled his hair up with sweat. He glanced back at his mother, and she looked forlorn, changed, even in sleep. The star was heavy in his vision.

Back at the old flat, he had listened in on his mother and their neighbour, Fran, from his bed.

'That's how they raise their boys,' Fran's voice.

'I'm not going to let him go out of control. He's still a boy.'

'Thirteen, he would have already been initiated if his father was still with us.'

'There's got to be some control.'

Kela steadied his hand, put his foot down. The road bent with the bay, he could not see if the car was behind him.

'He hasn't struck you, has he?' Fran's hushed voice.

'He takes my wallet when he doesn't want me to leave the house. He moved everyone's things out of the garage one day into the neighbours' upstairs because it was going to flash-flood.'

'Did it?'

A pause. 'Yes. You remember that crazy storm? The worst we had. Our street always cops it, low-lying area.'

Kela drove faster. He was ready. He went roughly around a corner; he heard his mother stir. He thought about looking at her again but he couldn't lose his focus.

'He's a big boy,' Fran had said. 'He doesn't look thirteen.'

'He's gone through too much,' his mother said. 'And I'm losing him.'

The car was not unlike his bed in their old flat. He was steering them towards the star, towards his father.

S & J

Jaye calls to stop when I'm going full blow down the line and I press my foot down hard thinking I nicked a roo. The dust mushrooms up and at first I can't see anything. When it clears I see the bird standing in the road, pale and overdressed.

'Far out,' I say.

'Pop the boot,' Jaye says.

'Hold on.'

'You've already stopped.' She pats the radio as she gets up beside me. 'And put something else on, will you? Don't want them to think we're all bogans.'

Jaye walks up to the bird, smile on, arms out, and soon the bird's smiling, too, giving Jaye her backpack and following her to the car. Jaye gets in the back seat, and the girl does, too.

'Hi,' she says. German accent. 'Sigrid.'

'Hi, Sigrid,' I say. 'I'm Esther.'

'Es,' she says. 'Es and Jaye.'

'Yeah,' I say, starting the car up and veering back onto the road.

'I'm so glad,' Sigrid says, 'that I've finally met a real Aboriginal.'

Through the top mirror I see she has a hand on Jaye's shoulder.

'You must tell me everything, Jaye. Tell me all about your hardship.'

We pull up to a service station and Jaye steps out to refuel.

'She's very beautiful.' Sigrid sighs. 'Strong.'

I grunt and ask where she's headed.

'Exmonth. I think that's how you say it.'

'Exmouth. Like this.' I show my teeth. 'Well, you're in luck, because that's where we're headed, too.'

'I'm very grateful, obviously,' she says. 'Where are you from?'

'Brissie,' I say. 'Brisbane. On the other side, the east coast. A little south from there, Gold Coast area, that's my country.'

'Sorry?' she says. 'I don't know where that is.'

Jaye's walking back to the car.

'You're a nice golden colour,' Sigrid goes on. 'You look like you're from Spain, maybe. Your parents immigrated here, yes?'

Jaye gets in. 'Dinner, ladies.'

She unloads her hands of raisin toast and chips and Cokes.

Jaye and I stand leaning against the car in the night air outside her grandmother's house.

'I'm really not sure, Jaye,' I say.

'C'mon, sis. We can hardly toss her out, can we?'

'I thought she'd have somewhere to stay when she got here. That's what she said.'

'Well, she doesn't, and she's alright, so …' Jaye straightens up and walks toward the house. 'You coming, or what?'

The house is a low-set cottage off the highway, surrounded by bush. The rooms smell stale, but it's cosy. There's a fireplace. Out back the veranda is falling apart and you can barely see the washing line above the waist-high grass. Jaye's cousins have been using it as a beach house for years. Now it's her turn.

We eat on the veranda, and then Jaye digs out a bottle of vodka and a deck of mismatched cards. Sigrid teaches us a German version of Rummikub. I'm not drinking, but the night moves quickly, like a train passing stations without stopping. A large ringtail possum sits in a nearby paperbark, and Sigrid squeals when I point it out. She wants to feed it, but we have nothing besides our breakfast for tomorrow. Jaye teaches her the word for possum in Yindjibarndi, and then the name for the tree, and then the name for the one next to it, and I'm all too used to it by now and roll my eyes. When the possum skirts off I decide to do the same.

Underneath the sheets I flick around on my radio for a bit, trying to get a channel. I can still hear the clink of wine glasses and the low murmured laughter from outside. It's a hard decision, to gulp up sleep or stay awake for the morning light. I open the window and see a pink haze coming through. I like the thought of walking barefoot to the beach and out into the waves, but it would be strange to do it without Jaye.

I guess Jaye kind of dragged me along. I didn't want to be by myself at the house all semester break. Everyone else was going back to their families. I was the only one who lived near mine and didn't feel like sticking around. It's funny now, with the darkness and the silence, no lights, no parties, that Jaye seems more distracted. She's been on edge ever since we got here.

When we met I was a shy teen and it felt good to be going places. Doing things. She was darker than me and all the other Murris I knew, like a walking projection of what a blackfella was supposed to be like. She knew language, knew them old stories. Had to say 'deadly' every second sentence. Postcard blackfella.

At first I liked it. But lately she was becoming too much for me.

There are these sounds in the distance, like hooting, but it's not owls. I sit up. It's a horribly low sound. I look outside, but all I see is trees and mud and mangroves.

I pad down the hallway in my night-time thongs. The living room is dark, but they're sitting on the couch. They're sitting too close. I go back to bed.

The droning stops. I can hear some thumping around, still, and am about to sing out 'Quiet, you brolgas' when I realise the laughter in the living room has been replaced by weighted sighs. The door to the next room opens, and the bed springs pop. I can tell they're trying to be quiet, which is worse. My chest feels tight. I pull the sheets over my head.

When I rise at eleven the door beside mine is still shut. I put the kettle on and butter some bread and sit with my modest meal at the small round green table in the centre of the room. Uni results tomorrow. Let the envelope sit in my mailbox for a week. I started well. Gone to every class and that, read the textbook in advance, even. Jaye slipped me some of her work, but she let me stay rent-free. It was fine, for a while. At what point did I start doing more of Jaye's than mine?

She's left the keys on top of the television. Longboard under arm, I cross the road and walk down the path to the beach. I drag the lead through the sand, looking for an entry point between the bucketloads of kids. For a long time I stand between surfing and not surfing.

For lunch, I walk along the beach to the surf club and order some chips.

'You're not from here, hey?' the lady says.

'Yeah, how'd you know?'

The lady points to my Brisbane Broncos shirt. 'First time in WA?'

'Yeah.'

'Enjoying it?'

'Yeah.'

'There's this band on here tonight. We're expecting a crowd.'

'Oh, yeah – Milla Breed. My friend told me.'

'This is her last show. She's going to the States.'

'Good one,' I say.

Sigrid is in the living room when I get back to the house, reading one of Jaye's poetry books.

'Good morning,' she says.

'Hi,' I say. 'Where's Jaye?'

'Still in bed.'

'Okay.' I put the keys back. 'Last night, did you hear any noises – droning noises?'

'Not at all,' Sigrid says, amused.

'Right,' I say.

'You and Jaye are not ...'

I quickly shake my head.

'Good,' she says, and smiles.

'We still going to that gig tonight?'

'Es, I'm trying to sleep, eh.'

'It's 4.30 p.m.'

'You don't need to tell me the time. Hey, Sig's hungry. Can you get us a feed at the surf club? Something salty?'

At eight, the other door closed again, I pull on some jeans and the only closed-in pair of shoes I own. Flatten my hair.

When I get to the pub it looks like half the town's here, fishies and tradies. Everywhere we've been it's like a whole generation is missing. Haven't seen anyone my age since Perth, except the tourists. This last week every tourie and their dog wanted a picture with Jaye. Some wanted more than a picture. I'm always the one stuck holding the camera.

Mum used to tell me and my sisters when we were younger that being Murri wasn't a skin thing. But next to Jaye that was all anyone noticed.

I think of Sigrid. Should've known.

The lady from lunchtime is on the door. I give her a fiver to get in, and go to the bar to grab a drink. Milla Breed's all long black hair and long white limbs crashing on the stage. Her drummer can't keep up with her. I move

160

a little closer when she starts a new song, trying to catch a lyric, but the words are in and out so fast you can't grab 'em. They're more utterance than words. Reminds me of the droning from last night.

She kneels, hands out to the crowd, then gets up, hands back on her guitar. She's wearing engineer boots, a denim skirt and a black shirt. Sleeves cut off like Jaye's. Jaye likes all the grunge bands, especially the Aussie ones. She plays Breed's stuff all the time, except her third LP, which she reckons is womba. I usually stick to golden oldies, the Beatles and the Stones; Mum reckons I'm the only one she knows who likes both. But Jaye's right on this one. This bird is good at what she does.

'Hiya, Exmouth, how you doing?' she drawls.

'Show us your titties!' the big bloke in front of me screams, and I think she does but I can't see because my view is momentarily blocked.

'Get lost, dyke,' one of his mates says to me as I press forward, and I tumble back onto some bird's toe and scurry to find another place to stand.

The crowd sparks when Breed plays her radio hit as a closer. She sings it differently, addressing the room between verses. Then she slows down and flicks her hair up, gaze on mine, the blue-green of her eyes like a globe, and even though she must be forty-five, easy, I can't help but lower my own look, her breasts prominent in the muscle shirt. I don't need to think about what Jaye would say, because I'm thinking it. Too deadly.

She waves to the crowd and floats back behind the wall. I buy a record at the bar and wait awhile to see if she's coming out again, but they've got another band up, some father-and-son act, and they're playing Cold Chisel covers and all the blokes are mumbling along as if they've forgotten about her.

As I'm walking back up to the driveway a white taxi swings in front of me. Sigrid's standing there, her hair orange in the light.

'Where you going?' I call.

'Home,' she says.

I walk up closer.

'Sigrid?'

'Yeah?'

'I'm not from Spain. I'm Aboriginal.'

'I know,' she says. 'Jaye told me.'

I nod and watch her put her bags into the boot.

She turns back. 'You don't look it. But you probably think I don't look German, either.'

I walk inside and switch the light on. No sign of Jaye. I sit on the couch and try the remote, but the television doesn't switch on. There's a stack of papers beside the poetry chap-books, and I flick through a couple of *Koori Mail*s. It's a while before I realise I'm waiting for her. There are a few things I want to say, and I think I will say them.

The house is still. I go through the next stack. There is Breed, on the contents page. I flick to the double-spread interview.

My stomach rises with every word. She's talking about her childhood, her family. Blue eyes on the page. By the end of it I'm so worked up I stand and think about going back to the bar. She might still be there.

Car would be faster. I open the door and walk out to it. Start the beast and drop down the driveway. In my mind I'm walking up to Breed and she looks at me and doesn't say a word, just grabs a bottle off a chair by the throat and sucks it, looking at me still. She tells me that I'll do, pulls me to her small frame, and pushes my jersey up over my head.

I stay at the foot of the road, in the driveway. I breathe heavily. Turn the engine off.

Still no sign of Jaye inside, but there is the drone again. I open the screen door, and the sounds feel louder. Jaye's fluoro singlet is out back in the dark – she's in the yard with garden clippers and hasn't made a dent in the overgrowth.

'What are you doing,' I call, 'in the dark?'

She turns to look at me. I take a torch off the table and walk down to her. She looks at my hands and I realise I'm still carrying the paper with the interview.

'Didn't know Breed was a Koori,' I say.

Jaye says nothing.

'What's up?'

'The fuck have you been?'

'What? I was at the gig; I tried to get you up for it, but—'

'I told you yonks ago I didn't want to go. The chick's sold out, eh. Going to the US to be in a porno. Thought you'd left me, too, sista.'

'Sigrid?' I ask pointedly.

'Sig? She's just a chick, you know. You're my best mate. I thought that was the whole deal of coming here. I was

163

going to show you where I grew up, all them old spots, introduce you to my mob …'

'You're the one who stayed in her room all day.' It's hard to believe her when she says she wants me around. I feel pretty replaceable.

Jaye's head stays down.

I sigh in defeat and put my arm around her shoulders, sweaty and acidic. She stares out into the yard.

'Why'd Sigrid go?' I ask.

'Think it was you.'

'I thought it might have been those noises that scared her off. I reckon this place has ghosts.'

'What, that?' Jaye's laugh mimics the drones. 'It's just dingoes, eh.'

'We'll start tomorrow,' I say. 'Nice and early. Exploring.'

Jaye grunts. She looks at me. 'How was it, anyway?'

I'm not sure how to answer. 'Not the same,' I say.

At that moment the ringtail runs along the railing.

The Falls

The Villa mob were back from the city and back in their old place near the creek bed and everyone thought we should have a cook-up that night. Mum was making salad with her boomerang arm Dad had given her. Grace and I were on the couch waiting for Dad to come home. I looked at Grace's bright pink lipstick. Her eyes were like sizzling jewels brought to life. She was wearing a bold singlet and denim cut-offs shorter than our neighbour's two-year-old's. I saw under her hand on the other side of the couch she had her oversized New York T-shirt ready to change into, as if half-accepting defeat.

Dad walked in but didn't say anything. He didn't look at us and when Mum came over to greet him he backed into the bedroom and shut the door. Grace gave me a look and flipped open her hand mirror, checking her makeup. Mum had left the salad bowl next to me and I looked at the contents – the tomatoes red with energy, the onions peppering my eyes. It was about as beautiful as my mother. I was surprised to see her curled to the window, her back to us, watching the red dust tides.

We waited for Dad to come out of the bedroom. I didn't know what he was doing in there, or how long he'd be.

I thought he'd just need to take a piss and put on his favourite T-shirt that we got him for his birthday. Mum warned me not to go in but I went up and put my ear to the door. It was the only door in the house and it always held a fascination. I thought I could hear the hum of radio, though our radio had been broken for a year or more, that's what Dad had said, unplugging it and putting it under the bed for safe keeping. I rested my head on the ground and nudged my eye under the door. The bed was tucked up neat. Was my father under the sheets, wrapped up? I smelt cigarette smoke and peppermints – the strong kind he got from the petrol station.

I felt my hand crushed, and saw Grace standing on me. I yelped and quickly got up, calling her half-formed names.

'I'm not *stupid*,' she hissed in my face and gripped my arm. I pinched her and then the door opened and we withdrew from each other.

My dad had shaved his beard and moustache – it was the first time we'd ever seen him clean-shaven. He was wearing olive-green cargo shorts and a button-up shirt I had never seen him actually wear but recognised from the wedding photos of him and Mum.

He said nothing about Grace's outfit, maybe to discourage a comment about his own appearance, and as usual I was the one picked on. He put a hand on my forehead, almost covering my eyes and said, 'You mind your manners, tonight. Especially with them old people.'

I shunned a smart response, feeling my tongue seethe.

My mother came to our side and Grace flashed me a snide look that was better than nothing from her. Even when Grace mangled my hair it was better than being ignored.

'We ready?' my mother asked.

My father nodded and went outside to inspect the car. We had packed it this morning – after the cook-up we'd leave as a big mob for the falls, stay there until Sunday and then head home in time for the kids to go back to school. Our car was packed up like a real blackfella's car, dirty mattresses flapping out of the window, unregistered plates, red dirt and rust on the bonnet. All someone needed to do was give it a paint job proper way – dots and that.

My mother was watching my father checking the water level under the bonnet.

'He'd be too hot in that shirt, eh?' she asked us, to make sure she wasn't the only one seeing what she was seeing. Grace made a vague noise of agreement. Of course he'd be hot, it was January, school holidays. The time of year where we spent our days with our eyes on the clouds, hoping they'd live up to their promise. Mum went back in the bedroom and emerged ten minutes later, holding a grey T-shirt but frowning as if she couldn't find the one we all knew as his favourite. 'I'll bring this,' she said, folding it up into a small square and slipping it in her bag, the one the women had weaved for her. I picked up the salad bowl and carried it out to the car.

Grace and I walked to the Villa place. When we got there the place was really full with mobs of people. I saw the kids my age first, sitting by the Esky with the fizzy drinks. The kids Grace's age were listening to music from one guy's big red headphones, and I maybe had heard the song before; maybe Grace had let me listen to it on one of those nights Mum and Dad were out and she'd let me sit on her bed and tell me the story of Grandmaster Flash, how he got his name, he was an electrician.

I saw the old ones look at us, and I was shy. Mum grabbed me by the hand and said, 'Give Aunty Elaine a kiss and Aunty over here. Go and show them who you are.'

When the women kissed me I felt like I'd been turned into a boab tree, their skin was deep and I felt myself shrivel up. I didn't like talking about myself. Sometimes they'd want to know whether Mum had taught me how to make quandong jam or how I was going at school and sometimes they'd forgotten my name and thought I had a brother but they were interested in me all the same. They touched my hair and gave me hugs that crushed my ribs. After I had been there for long enough they switched into language, my ears would skip over and I looked down at the dirt.

The adults were playing Country and Western, though I could hear some beats in the corner. Grace was there with a group. I went over, beside two of the Villa kids, Joanne and Dec.

'Hi,' Dec said to me, smoothing his long hair back behind his ears. I didn't know how his hair was so straight. He was looking at Grace and Grace was looking at him in a way that was predictable for me.

'So how come you're back?' I said. Grace gave me a sharp look like a slap.

Joanne said, 'Dec went to lock-up.'

'Yeah,' Grace said. I could hear her heart hammering out of her singlet top next to me.

'Cars.' Dec half-smiled. 'And a few bottle-os and that. Now we're back here.'

They got to talking about songs they liked, Dec was talking about Dr Dre. Grace signalled at me to leave.

'I know that stuff too,' I protested.

'Shit, man,' Grace said. 'She's only ten years old.' And they all laughed.

'Go on,' she said, drumming her fingers, pointing them in my ears and in the direction of the younger kids.

I knew Grace wouldn't tell anyone, but she'd been training me up. She was serious about touch football. We'd take it out the back and when I had the ball she'd sing out, 'Go on, run at me, see if you get past me.' And I'd run some, the footy heavy, almost slipping off my chest and I'd try to be quick and dodge her but somehow I'd charge right into her and she'd hit me like she was a concrete block and I'd go straight to the ground, remembering to still hold the footy and she'd scream at me and press my ear into the inside of my arm. There wasn't much point in telling her there was no tackles in touch. She said to me, 'They're not letting me play footy. But next year, I'll be in with the boys. I'm better than them.' She easily wrestled the ball out of my grip, her nails needles, grazing my face as she got up. She kicked the ball so close to my skull I felt my head blow. It could be difficult to get back to my feet, still finding it hard to breathe, but I would watch her kick and chase the ball without a care – as if she'd run across all three deserts, no problem.

★

Food was the best thing about gatherings, I reckoned. I walked to the food table, keeping a lookout for Dad. I got in trouble for eating too much at these things. He said I ate *more than my share*. I had to *wait for the Elders* and it *wasn't my place*.

The barbecue smell brought warmth to my cheeks. There was no sign of Dad with the other men. Mum's vibrant salad wilted next to the corn chips, rice crackers, dip, sausages, sticky chicken sticks. I eyed off the food. Dad and Grace usually hit me before the food did. But they weren't there to stop me and I stood for a little while at the table, feeling like the fifteen-kilos-overweight ten-year-old I was. I picked up a kebab and took a bite, the satay sauce running down my lips and onto my shirt, an old one of Grace's. Caught, I put down my paper plate and the rest of the chicken stick. The party and people went on without me. I saw my mother side by side with the other women. They were encouraging her to dance to the music and it didn't take much until she was moving her bare feet on the dirt with them, a smile slinging to her face. I felt it as she looked over at me and I felt like running to her and kissing her hands and she was mouthing some words to the song I didn't know but understood as 'I'll look after you'. I forgot about Dad and Grace and the shame job. I piled up my plate and went to sit down.

My dad didn't seem to be minding his manners. He was normally so tight with the mob. It was a shock to see him sitting by himself on a deck chair drinking a can of beer. He'd come into the feed aggressively friendly as if he'd wanted to put people off from mentioning his cleanly shaven profile. Like those teenagers who come home from the city with edgy haircuts and eyebrow piercings, looking at you like, 'I dare you to mention it, kid'. My father had slipped, like the time he rolled his ankle at the Bungle Bungles and he went down like a lizard in a hole.

'How's the salad?' Mum said. She'd come over to fix my hair, sprung up with the endless ruffling.

'Great, Mum.'

'Good. Make sure you get 'em greens into you, girl.'

I missed my dad's loud voice in the mix. His stories of roo-hunting and tourists in trouble. I wanted him to laugh. Before I was born, and a few years after, when Grace and I were too young to remember, Dad worked as a diver and they lived in Broome. When they moved here, he got a job at the council, working different jobs. I don't know as much about him as I do about Mum. Grace reckons he can't read but we should never tell him we know. Grace says he's not too nice but we don't choose our fathers.

That night a lot of mob talked to me but mainly I circled through the stations of Dad and Mum and Grace. By the time it was 9 p.m. and the sun had set, Dad's shirt was soaked at the sides from the armpit and at the neck. Mum looked worried about Dad but she didn't go over there, no one did, because he had found an old newspaper and held it close to his face.

'Mad sounds,' Grace was saying, her head bumped up tight against Dec's, the red headphones tying them together.

I wanted to stay awake for the ghost stories but I didn't make it.

Mum or someone must have carried me to a sleeping bag and I came to this conclusion jolted upright by Grace sneaking in beside me, a lo-light torch strapped to her wrist. Before we lay down, Grace's head by my feet because she said I gave her nits, she pointed the torch in my eyes and said, 'He's so into me.'

'What does it feel like?' I asked. I slipped a sock off my foot, and the cool air caught the pool of sweat between my toes.

She didn't pinch me for speaking to her. She just lay back and I could see her teeth and her eyes and she began to hum. This track I knew, 'It's Like That'. She stopped to say, 'Phew! That reeks, man. Put your socks back on, you idiot.'

We woke up at dawn, the kids shaking the bugs out of the sleeping bags onto each other, the grown-ups looking worse than last night. We ate cold sausages and onion for breakfast and there was leftover cream cake, too, if we remembered our toothbrush. We went to the cars. There were hugs and kisses to make your back hurt even though it was only a two-hour drive to the falls. Mum and Dad and Grace and I squeezed our butts into our car, the seats already burning with a day that had started without us. Dad seemed okay now and Mum had brought coffee for him and her in a thermos. Grace asked if she could have some and Dad said yes. He took his shirt off and hung it in the window to keep the sun out of our eyes.

The Wheel

If you drive out past the one-pump service station on the edge of town, where the new dirt reaches the old dirt, out where there's nothing but fresh countrymen's land, that's when you see the wheel. In the pale echoic distance, a thin impending structure that fascinated us as kids. Don't ask me how long it's been there. All I know is you'd be hard pressed to find anyone from here that doesn't remember it.

Small community, and my sister told me what she thought I needed to know about it. The best time to nick lip gloss from the shop – after a dust storm, when the woman's still cleaning her glasses. Where to take a boy if you like him. Sometimes she pointed things out and didn't say anything, like the glimpse of deckchairs under thickset trees behind the post office.

My sister and I used to count the kilometres and calculate how far we'd get if we ran away. I grew up knowing the distances: 250 ks from the ocean; 400 ks from the nearest major town, Broome; 2500 ks from Perth; 1500 ks from Darwin. We wondered how far we'd get before someone would notice and people would start looking. Soon the word would spread, jump from town to town, and we'd be the black girls everyone'd be talking about. How much chocolate would we need? I used to ask Grace. Could I be the one to choose?

This was on the afternoons when Mum wouldn't talk, and Dad would be out the back, in the shed, and we would hear him shouting, hitting things.

The first time I saw it happen I was in the kitchen, filling in my spelling sheets for class at the table. Mum came in from outside. Dad had been spending a lot of time in that shed. She didn't look at me as she turned on the tap, filling the sink for the dishes. We heard him, and I didn't quite believe it. It sounded like something happening from another family. Wood against metal. Man against the world. I was shocked but my mother didn't seem shocked.

My mother started crying. She put a hand on her temple, bowed her head and started sobbing. To comfort my mother wasn't a natural instinct. I'm not sure if she had a shield around her or if I was too young to contemplate that she might need me for something. So instead of going to her and holding her I moved to leave.

'Stay. Keep doing your homework,' she said in a thin voice. Her elbows were shaking but she still scrubbed the plates.

One day Grace came at my mother with the Broome phone book open to mental health services. This was a few weeks after he had stopped working.

'Your father won't go,' Mum said.

'Yeah, but we can get Uncle over there—'

'No. This is between us. It is a family matter.'

'When did they stop being family?'

My mother shook her head. I realised she never really let anyone in, not enough.

That year there was a new girl in town and when Grace and I went to meet her Grace said, 'What, did your parents leave you in the bath too long?' She was so small she came up to Grace's hips.

She wore ribbons in her white-blond hair and had glasses with a gold and purple butterfly on them. Her name was Stephanie Grey. She looked too young for the age we knew her to be, she was in my class, composite grade six and seven. Her ideas came from encyclopaedias. She owned a complete set – I saw them in her room when I went over there.

'We're from Melbourne,' she told us.

'Solid,' Grace said. 'That's a long way. Crossed a few countries to get 'ere. You'd be hot soon, eh.'

'I am already,' Stephanie said.

Grace had started a hip-hop crew who hung out at the skate bowl on a Friday night. They were responsible for the town's graffiti tags, and the blaring music after nine.

She had quite a following of younger girls – they all looked up to her, what else was there to do – and Stephanie was one of them. I felt sorry for her. Things could've been different for her, if she hadn't been blinded by Grace.

When Stephanie saw Grace dance in assembly, she stood up and clapped her hands, made a big scene and that, and we all stared at her. We were the casual breed. Serial under-performers and undertalkers, jeered at by teachers who thought of us as no-hopers, destined to be dole bludgers and, if we were lucky, tradies or kitchenhands. We didn't like outspokenness, hand raising, blowtorching.

Stephanie thought Grace was the deadliest. She followed her home after school whenever she could, and that's how she became my friend.

My sister and I lay down in the bed we shared.

'Why can you feel your heart in your arm?' I asked.

'It's your pulse,' she said, pushing me off her.

'Why is it in your arm?'

'If you ask me one more question I'll give ya an arm like Mum's got.'

'That's not nice,' I said.

I caught a glimpse of regret flash across her face before she pushed her palm into my nose and put her headphones on. Dad had been onto Mum again, like he did when we were little. I don't remember but Grace does. Abruptly, she grabbed me in a headlock. Her hands lodged through my hair, breaking knots.

'Geez. You look like no one owns you. Your hair's a fucking nest. When was the last time you washed it? Or ran a fucking comb through it?'

'I don't have a brush. Mum was going to get me one.'

She sighed – it was painful for her to say, 'Use mine.' She got it out of her studded toiletry bag. 'Rinse it after, though. Wash it good, otherwise I'll kill you.'

Mum wasn't home much. She had found the deckchairs at the back of the post office. Where they'd got the grog in.

Secret grog business. She'd come home, at eight or nine at night, when dinner had been forgotten. With a scent I didn't know yet, but Grace said, 'You reek of fucking gin, Mum.'

Grace and Mum were always fighting. 'You're a disgrace,' Grace said. 'You're embarrassing. It's about time you looked after us.'

It just wasn't in her power. She couldn't be a great provider on twenty dollars a week. She had given up. About once a fortnight Mum came home with supplies, but we would eat the good shit in a day. I learnt to pinch food. I helped myself to a lot from the school tuckshops, from friends' places, from the footy club.

The smell of Mum's alcohol became a comfort to me – the way it reached to my fingertips and my hair.

That next January I started bleeding and like usual Mum and Grace weren't home. I began to notice the distances between us: 200 ks between Grace and Mum, 100 between me and Mum, 3000 between Dad and Mum. I gasped as I sat upright on the toilet, hugged my arms around my chest, sat there for an hour but there was no one to come.

I tapped on the shed door. 'Dad. I know you're sick, eh, but I need help and you're the only one who's home.'

He opened the door and his expression changed when he looked at me. This was the first time I'd seen him properly for months, more than the moving figure between hallways, limping in the yard. He was skinnier. He was going bald. His chest hair was uneven.

'Second drawer in the bathroom. You'll find it there.'

I came back with tweezers, cotton balls, kids medicines. Nothing for a girl on the verge of womanhood.

This time he didn't open the door the whole way. 'Go to one of your friends. Tell her mum you got the monthlies.'

I walked to Stephanie's house. Her mother was helpful, in an artificial way, as if she was being careful for me not to get attached. Their bathroom was spotless and dry, looked like no one shit in there. I cleaned myself up and went out into the living room. Stephanie's parents didn't want me hanging around, and I didn't want to stay either. Stephanie put a book in my palm. She said it was for Grace.

I got home. Mum wasn't there. The fridge was empty. Dad was swearing loudly outside, above the droll beat of the insects. Grace was on the bed, angry. 'I can't take this anymore,' she said. She scratched the scars on her knees she got from breakdancing.

'Let's run away, like we said.'

She nodded. 'Yeah, alright, little sis. I said if it ever got this bad, we'd go.'

She got up and pulled her jeans out of the cupboard. Stashed in the back pockets was all the money she owned, fifty-four dollars, fifty-five cents. She took out a ten-dollar note and gave it to me. She took another ten and said, 'I'm going to the shops, get a few things. And I gotta see a friend.'

'Don't tell anyone, Grace.'

'I won't, stupid. Stay here and get ready.'

Hours later it was dark and our place still held the same number of occupants, no one had come home. Around midnight I walked myself to the skate bowl. There was Grace, sitting on the top of the ramp, kissing a boy. She had betrayed our plans; she was not coming. So that's how I ended up with Stephanie.

In the morning I was knocking hard at the Greys' front door. They were the only family that kept it all locked up.

'You're here again,' her parents said warily.

I pulled Stephanie into her bedroom, sealed the door closed with her stack of encyclopaedias, and told her the plan. She'd overheard Grace and me talk about it a few times when we were all together. She knew the plan better than I did, like the plot of her favourite *Famous Five* novel. It wasn't easy convincing her to come, and I almost felt bad. But her parents wanted to move back to Melbourne already; it hadn't worked out for them here, they'd said. And Stephanie wanted a story to take back there.

Our packs were light at first. I squeezed next to the Greys' fridge, inspected the contents, chose the orange-flavoured poppers Stephanie had in her lunchbox, crackers and cheese packs, Up&Go. When I walked out of town for the first time and out of the shade, I can tell you that I felt weightless. Stephanie didn't even need to be there. We headed east, deciding to follow the road for a bit. It was still school holidays and it would be a while until anyone noticed we had left.

We were in good spirits early on; I showed Stephanie a desert gecko curled still on a rock and she pointed out a collection of bike tracks someone had left. We must've looked silly starting off, a chubby black girl and a skinny white girl with backpacks walking along a few metres from the road. We only saw one car. We saw it approaching for a while, and we kept our heads down but it didn't stop. After that we walked a little more quickly, and there was a bit more grass up ahead. I walked through it. It was the last grass we saw.

Flat country here, eh. I knew it, couldn't help thinking if we walked far enough in this direction, we'd see the wheel. The wheel is where every kid wants to get to. We don't know how it got there, an abandoned ferris wheel erected in the middle of the desert. I knew if we made it to the wheel we would have done alright.

I quickly grew tired in the backs of my legs. The ground was tougher than I thought it would be. We had to look where we were walking. Stephanie was okay, being a talker. I got her to tell me about Melbourne. She told me a story about an African boy she once met on the bus. He didn't know where he was going so he had already been on seven bus routes that day. Stephanie explained that there are a lot of different buses in Melbourne. Like hundreds. All with different numbers and routes. The boy thought he would eventually get to where he wanted by chance. But in his hop-on, hop-off approach, every bus he took was taking him further from his intended destination. I wanted to know whether he got there, but Stephanie shook her head.

It was hotter than I'd imagined walking endlessly in the sun. 'Mum and Dad don't like me going outside.' Stephanie's face was smudged pink. Freckles sprang up on her arms like frogs at wet season.

I ripped a part of my backpack to make a hat for her. I laughed when she put it on. It kept falling off until she got the hang of walking in a careful way, her palms outward and her legs close together.

We made each other silly, inventing games to chase away the boredom. In between, when there were silences (they were inevitable, even with Stephanie who could chat about anything); I swore at Grace under my breath. She could get stuffed.

In the late afternoon we came to a small rock formation, barely taller than Stephanie, and after asking permission aloud I got up and stood on it, trying to see the wheel. There was a thick smudged dot beneath the cloud but it had no definition. Darkness fielded the sky.

We spent our first night cold. We had run out of food. I craved a bag of chips from the store. Stephanie was tired. I had got us settled between the rocks, using the backpacks as softeners. Stephanie breathed consistently from her nose. I couldn't get to sleep for a while. I felt my skin blend and burn with the familiarity of the rocky hill.

In the morning we trekked through the desert, and we got a few hours in before our bodies remembered they were wanting. We tossed around the aluminium water bottle like pass-the-parcel, until there was nothing but a metallic wink at the bottom. My cheap-arse shoes were cuffed at the sole already. I felt faint, but I was sure I didn't look half as bad as Stephanie, her face was a hollow glowing red.

'How come Grace didn't come?' she asked.

'I don't know. We're better off without her.'

She scrunched up her eyes in her glasses. 'Grace would have known what to do.'

I picked up a rock and raised it at her and she blinked and I knew this was not what I wanted to do, not how I wanted to act. I saw Grace, sitting on the ramp, talking to the boys, flicking back her dyed red hair, rapping, 'I don't fight with my fists, I fight with my words.' I thought of her secret tattoo. I saw it when she changed her shirt before bed. I didn't see it every night because she'd call me a pervert. A black hand, on the cave of her lower back.

I sighed. 'I wish Grace could have come, too. But she's not here.' I thought of what my mother said often. 'And we're going to have to do without.'

With the rock in my hand I went searching for food and water, Stephanie behind me. There had to be something still with me, my father's words, the years we camped with the other kids and mob from all over.

I hadn't talked for hours and when I opened my mouth my lips peeled off each other and throbbed. 'I came from here. I need to know how to survive.' I didn't expect or want Stephanie to hear me, but she was right behind me.

'I know how to survive in Melbourne. Catching trams and wearing four layers in August.' She giggled, and she laughed a little too long for me to think she was dehydrated.

Stephanie was fading when I saw the wheel piled under the clouds, close. I pulled her to her feet, spat on the blisters on her toes.

Although it looked close, I knew it would take us hours to get across.

I pulled Stephanie along, only looking at the wheel. I felt a hard pressure in my chest. The wheel was the only infrastructure in the frame. All day there had been no roads or buildings or people visible to the naked eye. Even the lizards didn't live here. I drooled my dry tongue down my shirt.

Stephanie's hand stuck in mine. I looked in her eyes, and saw the red lids. The women I saw at Ceremony travelled this journey every year with each other. I didn't know if I was on the ancestral track.

I felt Grace's presence overwhelmingly as I made those steps. She was a lift for me. Stephanie and I were still clutching at each other's hands. I longed for my mother's touch, Grace's tug at my hair. The rebelling feeling I had when I'd first set off had gone, replaced by a feeling of stupidity, of pointlessness.

I pushed this to the side when I realised Stephanie must be carried. I knelt down and gently hoisted her up. She was barely heavier than the backpack I used to wear, long left behind, but she was still a weight, and I had to learn to move with her. To feel the life force of someone else so close to me made me think of these women and all the years they'd lived this way.

We got closer until the old ferris wheel rose above us, spread out like a giant spiderweb. I felt out of my body when I stood, almost directly under the wheel. To have made it this far felt like something useful had been achieved, like an adult in a sail boat, sails raised against the sun. Though for us, maybe it was the feeling of *together*. A sort of vitality. The feeling of a new part that felt like home, a hill, or tree, a nut opening in your hand after breaking the casing.

I took Stephanie damply off my shoulders and felt us sink down into the earth in exhaustion. After resting there for a while I heard the sound of water and I lifted my head up in shock. It was coming from the base of the wheel. There was a tank and I could hear it pumping water up. I walked over – opened it and was dizzy at the enormous sight of the pale water inside the white tank. Gallons, it must have held. I put the bottle in and filled it. I went over straightaway to pass water to Stephanie, who was just strong enough to accept it without me helping her. We gulped down the liquid, swapping the flask back and forth.

It wasn't long until Stephanie's eyes grew huge at the sight of the wheel. She just couldn't wait to get up and sit in one of those carts. After another drink I joined her, climbing up the base and into one of the elevated ones. The seat was surprisingly cold, melting the heat of my shorts. The cart had rusted, white metal dissolving into red. The wheel creaked in the breeze, and the cart rocked forward and back a little, as if phantomly operated, as if ghosts were here, old people opened up by the lines of the giant circle cut across sky and land. I curled my chin into the cool face of my knee and looked out, taking in the view. This is the position I stayed in for several hours. My legs hardened from the effort. Stephanie had no words. We had found water and refuge but there was no food and I soon felt ill.

The sun set over the wheel. I got sicker pretty quickly. I had moved past being empty and faint, to a sort of violence. I lay on my stomach in the cart and threw my guts up over the side, onto the ground. What had got hold of my body was winning. I wondered about Grace and Mum and Dad and whether they were worried about me. Now I wanted them to come to get me. I wanted to be rescued. I imagined hearing the burst of an engine, Grace rolling through the dust in her boyfriend's stolen car. Better still, an ancient bus, the lettering on the front flickering like lightning. But it was Stephanie who got me through, she saved my life. She laid me on my side. She climbed up higher on the wheel to look out all around us and she found where the road would be. She's not just book smart. She ran almost all that way – there were cars going up and down looking for us and she got them moving towards me. She said it was 'a miracle'.

I woke up in Broome hospital. Mum and Dad had come as soon as they found out, thinking I may never wake up. But the doctor pumped my body with saline and potassium and I came out of it.

When I started to feel better I asked for Grace. My parents told me, but it wasn't until they took me home that I realised the truth: Grace had gone, too, but she hadn't been found. Her friends said she had taken off with Dec in a stolen Camry, she hadn't left a note. What I didn't figure out was whether she had gone before or after me. I didn't want to believe she had chosen her opportunity when her sister was lying in a diabetic coma. Dec and her were really in love, everyone said. Gonna get married. They weren't seen in Broome, and people thought they went the other way, across the border.

One of the first nights back home there was a real ripper of a storm. Our shanty flashed with the force. The small community, already in strings, was blown almost apart. A week of rain and the dirt I had walked in, I had known, turned to swampland. I thought of Grace, dreamed shelter for her, pathways where the storm couldn't fit, hidden patches of earth where even a season's rain couldn't touch her.

She was one distance that never left me.

Currency

Park drives his family out of the city. Connor sits on his mother's lap in the back, next to sports bags piled on top of each other up to the window. They reach the outskirts of the city, spread-out, fragmented, less sense to the order of things. Connor looks at the petrol stations, car yards, rubbish tips. Park doesn't stop. The landscape is changing too, drier earth, mountains ahead. Connor watches his father rush, and he is scared. His mother's knees are tighter than usual, and she says nothing to Park as they reach the edge.

Now they only pass highway rest stops and pie shops. At the rust colour in front of them, Park lets out a breath. Here, there is no longer the city's taste, the city's influence, the disease. His family will be safe. He squeezes his eyes shut for a moment. Blue notices cut-open earth often, unmanned machinery. They were drilling here.

Connor is hungry, and Park reaches in his pockets and passes Blue a small nectarine. The habit of Park to carry fruit with him never ceases to amuse Connor and his mother.

Park pulls up at a petrol station, the petrol startlingly cheap. He puts the pump in, Connor watching with intensity from the window. Park rubs his hands on the back of his jeans. He walks inside, there is an older man and a woman by the counter.

'You come in from the city?'

'Yeah,' Park says, paying.

'Day trip?'

'No. We're heading to Boom.'

'Visit?'

'Stay.'

'You got to know it's a lot different out there. Not what you'd expect.'

Park shakes off the caution. They must've picked him from the city clothes, he thinks as he walks back to the car. Park wears a white shirt with a print and sunglasses and jeans. Blue also wears jeans and a V-neck shirt, one of the ones she wore when she was breastfeeding.

Why Boom? He'd seen the place somewhere, on a map or a brochure. A mate worked there once, years ago, he was dead now. Park knew it was a few days away. He'd been looking for a name on the map, in the desert stretching across the paper. Something to reach for; but truth is, he was glad to find anything. There were jobs, he'd heard. In the mines. He'd be off for a while, and Blue and the child would stay put. They'd be safe, they'd find a house and he'd find the time to fix it up. Perhaps Blue could grow something.

Park swears under his breath at the state of the road. He lets out a warning when he nears a bump.

It is Connor who notices a track of camel dung. He glimpses the piles in wonder, and feels a smile pass over his lips. His parents don't notice.

Just looking at the desert outside the window makes Blue hot. It is so bright, yet so dull. A while passes on the road after the petrol station, quite a long time without seeing anything. Then they all sight the great-sized creature in the distance and talk at once.

'What is that?' Blue asks.

'Don't worry,' Park says, keeping his eyes on the road. 'Camel. There's heaps around here, apparently.'

'Hon, it looks strange. It has a horn.'

They pass it at the same speed and Park isn't looking back. Connor and Blue turn around, the boy's knees on the seat, watching it grow smaller. It is moving slowly, and horn or not, the sight of it makes them feel something that stays with them.

Park isn't going to mention what he's also heard, about the killer camel breed. Ones in particular they want to cull. He knows the gun is there in the dash.

Hours pass until they come across a small town, and Blue says softly, 'You want to stop here, Park?'

He hasn't thought of stopping, his grip tight on the steering wheel, but she brings him in, he loosens and becomes aware again of her and Connor in the back seat.

He nods and slows the car, finding a place to leave it on this main street of sorts. There is a small pub and a park and little else. And people. Blue smiles.

Park looks straight at the pub, a dry thirst on his mind. Blue tells him she wants to take Connor to the toilet at the park, and she'll meet him in there. Park stretches out his back.

He lopes in, hands on his hips. It is dark and there are a few odd-looking people about. He sees, and knows from experience, that at least one of them is carrying a gun. He asks the bearded barman, 'What you got? What beer?' The man points. Park digs into his jeans for his wallet.

'Nah, mate.'

'What do you mean?'

The man refuses to serve him. Park feels humiliation grow on his cheeks. The other people in the bar look over at him with a roughness in their eyes, stopping him from tempering over.

He walks out of there, finds Blue.

Blue looks across parched dry country. Although dull, there is a contrast of colours, between the deep dark blue of the range and the pale pink desert dirt. There are a few trees here, eucalypts. Connor points out a bird. The bird flies straight across the park – straight as an arrow. Then it floats delicately to ground.

There is a brick toilet block, with children's art on the gate. She takes Connor in. When they come out he wants to stay for a moment, his eyes following dragonflies hovering above the grass. They walk deeper into the park.

Blue thinks even the bark on the trees looks parched. There is a small creek bed, mostly dry. Above them five ducks fly across – their brown-and-white speckled bodies in formation. It must be good for Connor to see nature. She sits him down on her lap under the trees and they look out.

The metallic glistening of cars up the hill is the only shine. She wonders if it's a car yard. Could Park get a job there? She'll tell him. The quiet is broken into by the rasp of a motorcycle somewhere. More signs of life, for the family's future.

Park explains to Blue what happened in the bar and she puts a hand to his shoulder and says she would like to go in there. He looks back at the pub and says they should just leave, but she convinces him by gesturing at Connor, saying he will need a break in the cool, and a drink of water or Cola.

'I'll sort it out,' she says to Park and he follows her wordlessly, Connor by his legs.

When she gets inside she stands back a little and takes it in, as she is used to doing. The decor is rough, thoughtless. She watches the bar. The bearded man serving doesn't look up. There are a few men sitting around in a circle. She notices, surprised, that there is no cash register. She sees one of the men sitting in the middle is talking animatedly. She can't keep up with the flow of it.

When he finishes all the men cheer and stomp their feet and the barman pours a beer in a glass and pushes it across the counter. No money changes hands.

'Do you know where the river got its name?' the barman turns to ask her.

She shakes her head. 'I would like a drink, for my son. How do I pay?'

'Around here, with a story, love. You got any?'

She thinks he is joking. She stares into his eyes.

'Blue,' her husband calls behind her. He is tensed at the window, holding Connor by the hand. 'Let's go.'

★

They walk down the street as a unit, looking around the township, keeping to the shade. Park lights up a cigarette. Blue watches Connor suck another nectarine found in his father's pocket, the nectar blending into the sweat on his upper lip. They stop to look at the saw mill, peering over the fence. A man emerges wearing a singlet – he has a heavy gut and a sunburnt, smiling face.

'How you going?' he asks. A fly studding his cheek.

Blue talks for them. 'Good, and how are you?'

'Not bad, not bad. You see that huge tree over there? The red gum on its own? A man once lived in it, many years ago.'

'Really?' Blue says.

'Yep. He was wanted by the coppas for tax fraud, and he had no money, so he packed a bag and walked to the tree; see the opening at the bottom? He stayed there for two years before anyone figured it out.'

Park, who's been listening, lets out a low whistle.

'True,' Blue says. 'What happened to him?'

'So he'd been spotted stealing milk from the farmers. The authorities surrounded the tree and told him if he didn't come out they'd cut the tree down – and he was outside in a flash. He loved the tree, see. The moment he got out a huge branch fell with a crash, and narrowly missed the people below. Among the possessions he left in there was a dog-eared copy of Shelley's *Frankenstein*. He was sent to jail, but he was only in for a few months, a lot less time than he'd been in the tree.'

They walk nearer to the gum, marvelling at its size. Up close, with the texture of the trunk, the idea of a man living in it seemed tangible.

'You wouldn't have a smoke, would ya?' the man asks.

Park reaches into his pocket and under-arms the man the packet. 'Thanks.' He catches it one-handed. He lights up and waves, before he starts back into the mill, whistling as he goes.

They return to the car at nightfall. Park drives them a little bit further, imagining a place of safety as a bit off the town, but close enough for it to be a comfort.

There is a sliver of light behind them from the grid of buildings, and as the car rolls west there is nothing in front of them except bush entrenched in darkness. It is a darkness they are not used to. Park shoulders the car off the road. They pass around a torch as they peel out of their clothes into outfits more comfortable to sleep in. Blue gets the blankets out from under the seat and spreads them across the backs of the seats. Connor is little enough to fit under her arm as she lies down across the back seat. Park leans over his seat and plants a serious kiss on both of their cheeks, the whites of his eyes pinning into the darkness. When he shifts back into place he rests the gun between his legs and leans back. Inside the car all is quiet. Connor's short, sharp sucking sounds help Park keep time. A few of these a minute and Park feels his wife and child relax into almost sleep. He himself relaxes a bit in turn. He checks off mental lists of protection from immediate and far-away danger. All four doors shut. There's still the food left in the yellow bag and Connor's medication.

The lights from the town behind them have gone out. Park adjusts his back into the chair. There is a bump on the car, they are hit by something. And then something again. Park swears, springs up, Blue and Connor stir at the back.

'What is it?' Blue mutters.

Park tries to see out the window – points the torch at the glass, but he pushes back from the force of the thing or things hitting the car. He lifts the rifle and keeps it aimed. The car is rocked and Blue screams for him to start it. His hands are trembling too much; the next hit makes him move, he forces himself over the back seat, covering Blue and Connor, getting them down on the floor. A strong, distressing smell suddenly comes in his mouth, wet earth, undeniably camel. He tenses, waiting for the sound of smashing glass, for their safety to burst, but it doesn't. After a while it stops. Park gets up and shines his light at all sides, but he can't see anything.

In the morning, when Park inspects the car, he is shocked. As well as dints, and horn-shaped marks, he finds the back two tyres have been slashed by the creatures. He tries not to show all of his frustration; Blue and Connor are still shaken from the night, and none of them have slept much. Blue makes breakfast by mashing a banana onto grain crackers. They get dressed and start the walk to town. Park is adamant he won't leave them in the car, they are all staying together.

They are immediately unsettled by the terrain, and drained by the heat. Park carries a quiet Connor on his shoulders. He feels a wave of love for his boy; he would do anything. This time last week he was in the supermarket and he had seen a child his boy's age with lumps all over his face, sending him into terror. That afternoon he'd starting packing.

Outside the town, a group stands. Three men, all wearing broad-brimmed hats, are in the middle of the road.

'What should I say?' he says, turning to Blue. 'Will they help us?'

'Tell them about the tree,' Blue says.

Park licks the corner of his lips. He runs a line in the dirt with his toe and he moves towards the men.

He does not know he has a son who sees the camels in his dreams. They are honey coloured with two long horns, oldtime patterns on the backs of their necks and skinny tails. For this visualisation, he is one of them, sitting on the back of an old girl, and they will never harm him.

Sound

Nights blister my fears. One night I wake up to the phone ringing in my hand, buzzing blue. I am too hurled into dread to answer it before it stops. The numbers hold no recognition, no area code or spiritual repetition. 10.30 p.m. A late call. It must be him. Not him, someone who found him. Dead. Crazy. Both. The hospital, the police, one of his mates.

The phone doesn't have to ring for me to think those thoughts. Sometimes I can't sleep. But I feel guilty – today, I haven't thought of him at all. I had an assignment due, and I had a house inspection. I had even baked. Honey oat biscuits out of the oven, a little burnt. Warm things I had made that I put in my palm.

The number doesn't call back a second time. It takes me almost an hour to summon the courage to dial it back. Only two tries and I'm through. It is a media company wanting to survey me.

'How did you get my number?' I say, almost shout.

Still I can't sleep. I try putting the radio on, pull the volume down so only a sliver of noise enters my thoughts. Living in an apartment block alone sometimes feels like my room could topple backwards off the building and no one would notice. The seven-floor apartment block is a still thing, a lighthouse, and the sea beneath my window is an intangible space. They keep building up from the ground, soon there will be no green space to see, on a campus that used to be known for its gardens. I look into the face of the city and feel homeless.

My brother has been here only once, when I first moved in. He refused to come inside, simply standing at the door, muttering 'hurry up already' and tapping at the frame until I had finished getting ready. It had been my twenty-first birthday and we went out to dinner with our mother, a strange thing it had been, the three of us.

It is Friday night and late enough for me to be weary. I walk into the tavern; I'm wearing old jeans, a tired T-shirt I pulled out of the washing basket and tennis shoes in case they enforce closed-in shoes. From the look of it, I didn't have to worry. I see someone I know from high school wearing a pair of flimsy gold sandals. It is always a surprise to recognise a classmate, I push those years out of my mind. She is drinking with a table of other young women and men I don't know. This sort of thing is foreign to me, drinking with people on a Friday night. The tavern is crowded with mainly boys my brother's age. A band is playing downstairs later. Silvaspoon? Stain? Collide? I don't know the name, it is the sort of heavy metal band I've found out my brother liked. As is typical, they won't start for a few hours, and all the young men, in their early twenties like my brother, are drinking and talking with a sort of characteristic impatience.

I walk from one end to the other – outside, the balcony looks out over a golf course where punters take their hits behind a large net. Not surprisingly, I don't see him. But, like I hoped, I spot his friend Michael at the table near the railing. Michael has dyed-black hair, a nose piercing and is wearing a baggy white T-shirt with the band and a guitar graphic on it. He is holding a bottle of Stone's and is eating from a plate of nachos.

'Hi,' I say, and too late realise I have descended on him too eagerly.

'Hey, Jodie.' He keeps his eyes down.

'Have you seen Dave lately?'

'Not really.' He doesn't offer me a seat. The girl next to him looks me up and down suspiciously.

'So what are you doing here?' he asks.

I still a laugh, looking around. It is a good question.

'Just … getting a drink,' I say, playing it cool. 'Well, I'll go to the bar, want anything?'

'No, thanks.'

'Can I sit down here when I get back? Have a chat?'

'Umm … we're expecting someone but until he gets here, I guess that could be okay.' The girl gives me the look again.

At the bar I find myself in line behind the girl from school, and I have no choice but to acknowledge her.

'You remember me?'

'Yes,' she says, unsmiling.

There is a pause.

'What are you doing with yourself?' she asks.

'I'm doing my Masters. You?'

'I'm a real estate agent. You here to see the band?' That suspicious look.

'I'm looking for my brother. David. Do you ever see him?'

The girl shakes her head.

I am closer to the counter. What can I drink that I won't taste for weeks to come, like the rum cocktail from the student gathering in West End I should never have gone to? The girl from school orders a gin and tonic. I order the same.

Back on the balcony I ask Michael where David is staying. Michael says he doesn't know. Ask Dustin, he says. He doesn't know what days he works, either. 'I think he's alright, you know. You shouldn't worry about him.' The longest line Michael has given me. I wonder if he knows more than that, if he is capable of more. All these weeks of getting the same answers.

Then he looks behind me and says, 'Ry!' and I feel myself get up, grab my white bag from under the table and walk to the car park where I've left my bike. Between the tavern and the golf course is an expanse of gold-black grass, and I catch the movement of a rabbit on its way to the other side as I clip my helmet on. The laughter increases above me and the band is still hours off.

The supermarket shelves shine like bone. I stand where the meats are, facing the coldroom door. Every few minutes I feign interest in the chicken drumsticks or the two-dollar unlabelled mince, but the truth is, I'm vegetarian. A while back I saw a figure that could have been my brother, same build. Dark hair. I wait and think about what to do when he comes out of the door. What will he do? Will he ignore me like last time, walking faster with his long legs, a stride no one can match, going down the aisles dispelling bottles of milk into the fridge and then to the next checkpoint, shrugging off my questions until I feel stupid and fall back into a sense of intrusion? There is little point in saying hello, when he never answers greetings, or even pleasantries in phone calls, text messages, emails. And to interrogate would make him retreat. So what can I say – it's a good day outside and what did you have for breakfast and has it been busy? Have you got your tax file number forms done? No, too motherly. A cool, casual sister would tease him about his uniform, the gloves. No, I've tried that one already. He will just walk and keep walking. No calls of Snowman will slow him down.

He had grown taller quickly. The house became his. Sometimes he locked the doors, kept me and my mother out for periods of time. An annoyance. One day I got home from uni, my bladder close to full. I crept around the deck for a bit, calling his name. I got a metal spatula from the barbecue and started to pick at the lock.

'Jodie.' His voice came through the gap. 'Go away. I'm busy.'

'I live here, too,' I said, and I pushed the door open. When I saw him I knew he wasn't well, his hands were trembling and his eyes were rough and red but it was too late, he grasped the spatula out of my hand before I could react. I just looked at him. Three years older, I thought, why this fear. He pushed me against the door. He opened it and slammed it into my rib and I fell back on the deck floor. He kicked me again, and I had seen it before, but now, with the glass door in front of me, I was seeing it done to myself. At the third impact my bladder broke, hot spills of liquid down my thighs. I lay there, on my side, gasping but mute. I told him the next time, 'You got to stop. I'm your sister.'

I take a pile of unread overdue books back to the library on campus. I go up to the second floor to log on at a computer and check my emails. Two from my supervisor sent last week. I haven't sent him my proposal yet – last week he had said. I type sullenly back, *Can we meet?* I look at the time. I will leave soon. He wasn't there yesterday, so he must be there today.

The supermarket on a Monday afternoon is mainly mums and young children in school uniforms pushing the trolleys. I stand in my usual spot. Other workers walk past. How can they not know what he's really like? Why are me and my mother the only ones who know? Why couldn't he keep it from us like he could with others, who all say he's a gem of a boy, bright, albeit unmotivated. 'Lost' sometimes. I think I am about to cry when a young girl in uniform with fizzy orange hair comes up to me.

'He doesn't work here anymore,' she says.

I rode through the suburb, left notes, called into cafes, walked through apartment blocks. He was lost and didn't want to be found. I am his only family in Brisbane now. He is twenty and he must still need his family.

After he had smashed everything left – wood, walls, tiles – in the house we used to live, he had taken off. It has been two months since I last saw him. Every week I do the rounds. It astonishes me to think he may have made his way out of the suburb on his own, carless, when he'd never liked public transport.

I go to the old house, something I have done weekly, to pick up the mail addressed to him or my mother. I have left his mail untouched, a pile of it in my apartment, next to the TV. He's always been prickly with his privacy. But today I feel myself ripping open a bank statement in the front yard of this place now rented by another family. All the notes I sent – *Dave, I have your mail. Let me know when you want it.* If he asks about the bank statement I will say the postman opened it. On the top line is an employee payment, minimum wage. I look the place up on my phone.

A fish 'n' chip shop in Sandgate. He has gone back to the first suburb we lived in. Does he remember like I do, the nights on the beach? Trudging sand through the house and sleeping in our swimwear? Weekly tussles, pulling each other underwater, almost drowning each other. When Dad was alive. The fish 'n' chip place is on the corner where we lived. A Sandgate institution. We couldn't afford to eat there as a family, but Davey and I picked up ice-creams after school with money we got from who knows where. Davey collected bottle tops from the tables outside. He is returning to our old suburb. I've heard we all return to water sometime.

The fish 'n' chip shop is busy when I arrive and it is a while until I can make my way to the counter. The girl working is tall and thin with long dark hair swept back into a pony-tail. She looks around my age, perhaps older. She has green glasses with stickers on the ends and a long neck. She is wearing a black apron over a white T-shirt.

'Hello!' She is enthusiastic but genuine. 'What would you like?'

'I'm here to see my brother, David.' A phrase I have said many times, like an imprint. In times like these, I am nothing but his sister.

'You're David's sister?' The girl smiles. 'That's awesome. He doesn't work today, though. The one day! He'll be here tomorrow.'

The girl has a warm smile. 'Come tomorrow. He'll be here after eleven,' she chatters. 'If you have time. What's your name again?' It is a shock to see someone so helpful. It is as if she gets it, no explaining necessary.

'Jodie.'

'I'm Sarah. David will be sure to throw you some extra chips. Crispy ones.' She smiles again, showing dimples.

He dropped out of school when he was sixteen and I was so disappointed I rang the school, the principal – would anyone give him a second chance? He had missed too many classes, too many assignments, and I was left to wonder if I should have seen the warning signs more clearly. He hadn't been to school since March, and I had been consumed with my course. What was the point of me graduating with honours when I'd left him by the educational wayside? What was achieving when your family was sinking? At first it was pride. Don't be another statistic. Then, it was worry. He didn't make a secret of what he got up to with his mates.

The next day I get there early, and before the place opens. I sit on the beach. Sandgate pool is behind me, where we both learnt to swim through a school program. I have lost touch, can't remember the last time I sat next to water and felt it lick my toes like an unloved dog. I hold my shoes in one hand. The sun bows in front of me. There is no one around. I feel nervous energy. On the bike ride to Sandgate I had seen roadkill on the bitumen, the bright orange mess of a possum on its stomach. I'd automatically made a mental note to go another way home.

Sarah smiles at me. 'Hi, Jodie,' she remembers. 'I'll grab David. He's not busy.' She goes around the back. I hear talking and it is a little while before he comes out.

He stands there holding his hands together. I look him over. He frowns and brings his hand up self-consciously, shielding his face with his watch.

'Dave's in charge of the spiders — you know, fizzy and ice-cream. I loved them when I was kid. It was his idea to add it to the menu.' She talks to him and he responds, ignoring me, but I'm touched to see him smile at a person, engage meaningfully. All of his words are traffic for me, however: I only notice his face and his hands and his arms. Part of him looks different, as if a dog came back from a hydrobath, shaved. Exposed. I think of my mother and father. A customer walks in and I rush to say something, ruining the moment.

'Where are you living?' I ask him.

His head tilts to Sarah.

'I had a spare room, and I heard he needed a place.' Sarah points – 'I live in that little street, actually. The white house with the balcony and the yellow tree out the front. It comes in handy living close because most of the time we have an hour off between lunch service and dinner. We just go back and take a load off. I have a dog, a little beagle called Scary. He doesn't like being left alone much, I can hear him from the kitchen here sometimes. You like dogs, Jodie?'

'I do.'

'You'll love Scary. Hey, Dave?'

At that I know I won't be out of place if I go to the white house at 3 p.m. on a weekday and knock on the door. I dare not look at my brother to see what his face might betray. I am suddenly so full of hope that I ride home with energy and don't remember the dead possum. I even get some research done that night.

I can't imagine my brother living with anyone else. He has not learnt how to be an adult. He can't manage money or time or duties. As far as I know, he still doesn't have a tax file number. He can't communicate. He can't take responsibility for his actions. Living with him was living on edge. How can he not hurt the lives of the ones he lives with?

The house is on the left side of the road, and I get off my bike and walk it over to the gate. I can hear Sarah's voice from inside. The gate creaks open and I walk up the steps. It is a cute, chic place, the kind of place my brother and I couldn't have imagined living in when we were growing up.

The beagle whines from the side, a whimper that increases as I get closer. I see the thump of a tail through the slats.

Sarah greets me at the door and lets me in. 'I haven't been here long, so excuse the mess,' she says. 'You're going to see a lot of stuff. It's mostly my grandmother's.'

We walk into the small front room, full of clothes and knick-knacks on every surface, and into the kitchen, which is equally cluttered. Large open windows treat the room to sunlight. David is sitting there with an energy drink and his phone in his hand.

'She passed away last month.' Sarah is putting the kettle on.

'Hoarder,' David says, raising his eyebrows.

I watch my brother closely. He doesn't look up from his phone screen. He has changed out of his uniform – a red apron and a white shirt with black slacks – to a flannelette shirt and jeans shorts, and his knees bump against the table. He is awkwardly tall, has been since he was fifteen.

'Have you heard from Mum?' I ask.

'Nope,' he says, his fingers skimming the phone keypad rapidly.

'How have you been feeling?'

'Fine.'

Sarah moves beside him and says softly, though I can hear, 'Do you want some scrambled eggs?'

'I'm fine,' he mumbles as he looks up at her.

She walks back to the kitchen. 'Do you want anything, Jodie?'

'Just some water, thanks,' I say.

My eyes catch sight of the bookshelf next to an art deco armchair.

'You like comics?'

She smiles at me. 'Yes, I'm a massive nerd.'

'So does David.' I look across and see my brother has chosen that moment to slink off, the back of him darting down the hallway like a fish, a great white tuna tunnelling under.

The wallpaper is royal red like a theatre. There are photographs on every wall. I hear a door close. I get up and follow David as Sarah nods her head at me.

I knock once on the door, and I hear David walking around in the room.

'Dave? Can I come in?'

'Just a sec,' he says in a neutral voice, but I remember his tricks.

'Open the door, please,' I say.

'What do you want?'

'I'm your sister, Dave. I just want to have a chat.' My words hurt me, the recognition of the sister line.

The door stays closed. After a few minutes, I give up. 'Okay, I'm going to go see Sarah.'

There is a silence. I wonder if he worries about what I'll say to her. Is she important to him? But he doesn't answer.

Sarah is sitting on the table with her back to me, her hands plaiting her hair. I sit down beside her, trying to be unobtrusive.

'How did you go?' she says.

'He doesn't seem to want to talk to me,' I say quickly.

'He's a boy,' she says. I wish I hadn't said anything. She has finished her plait and puts her hands down.

'How has he been?' I ask.

'Good. It's been good.'

'I suppose he doesn't help you with dishes much.' I try to laugh.

'He's done alright so far. He's been training Scary. And takes her out quite a bit.'

I nod. How do I express my worries to her?

'Since I've find out I'm pregnant I've been trying to eat a lot of eggs. It's good for protein.'

'Yeah?' I say.

'And I've been drinking lots of herbal tea. Dave drinks it, too.'

'How far are you?' I say. There is no shape to her in the long grey dress, not that I can tell.

'Only seven weeks. I haven't told anyone, except my mum and Sharon, the manager at the shop. She's lovely. And my mum's excited.'

She touches her stomach and I shake my legs under the table, numb from the shock. Something twists in my gut.

'Let's take you to meet Scary,' she says, getting up. 'You've heard her.'

She opens the screen door and the beagle comes racing in, nose first. She spools around my feet. I pick up her wayward, jumping paws and she pushes her wet nose against the inside of my arm. Sarah steps between us to shepherd her outside into the yard, where there are planter boxes and pots with plants. The garden has a vibrancy, and I'm reminded I couldn't grow anything on my balcony at home. These last few years I've worried that my love for my brother isn't enough. I couldn't care for him. I gave up on him. I don't invest enough. Nothing is nurtured in my care.

Sarah bounces an old tennis ball on the pavement twice and then sends it spinning out onto the lawn. Scary willingly obliges, sprinting forward, though after a few rounds she goes to protect the ball in a far corner by the clothesline. The screen door opens and Dave comes out, hands in pockets. He heads over to play with Scary. He commands her to drop the ball, and shows us the tricks he's taught her.

'She's pretty good now, at listening,' he says. 'I get her a sausage roll sometimes, one for me, one for her.'

'You've always liked your sausage rolls, Dave,' I say.

'Scary is going to have a heart attack soon,' Sarah says.

Dave turns his back, suddenly closes off before he's opened up.

'Mum and Dad didn't let us have a dog,' I say to Sarah.

Until I moved out, I knew about every girl who had broken his heart. He told me nothing, but I gathered from the cars, the glimpses of awkward-looking girls on the street. I knew by absence, what he didn't say. The days he spent in bed with his headphones on.

Sarah is a year younger than I am but better spoken. Her pregnancy is often on my mind. I can't think of Dave without thinking of her, her soft voice, her narrow laugh, her hands across her stomach. The smell of her grandmother's house is of tea leaves and cat food. We exchange numbers before I leave, her handwriting smooth against the faded receipt for a textbook I bought this semester but haven't yet opened. I open the receipt, when I get home, and put the number in my phone.

Sarah calls me up and says she's not able to invite me over for dinner because they work every night, but on Friday she has a longer break, an hour and a half, and she likes to make an evening meal of sorts, even at 3 p.m. She likes to try out her grandma's recipes. Would I be interested in coming?

A routine is formed. On Friday afternoons, after I've spent the morning in the library, I ride to Sandgate to have a late lunch at the house with Sarah and David, who have just come off their shift for a break. David tolerates my presence. At the table he eats a sandwich Sarah makes him because he won't try her cooked food, and then he goes off to his room and his games console. When I ask Sarah if it bothers her, she says, 'Nope, I'm just glad he doesn't ask me to watch. So boring.'

Sarah has made us blue-pumpkin risotto, leek soup, fresh oysters, and rainbow trout from the shop. When I arrive she is already busy cooking, and the house is persuasive with smells. I don't eat like this at home. She uses her grandmother's place setting, beautiful bowls and serving dishes. They are heavy to carry back over to the sink. David's letters lie untouched where I put them on the side-table.

When we've eaten, usually Sarah and I take Scary for a walk on the beach, as she gets moody when she's cooped up. This is my one crowded hour with Sarah, and it leaves me wanting more.

After that it is late in the afternoon and I sit at the fish cafe, outside, while Sarah works at the counter and David in the kitchen. The sun sets behind the beach and the figures of the people walking by the water deepen into shadows. I speak to Sarah periodically throughout the evening. They get quite busy with groups sitting down or getting up. I concentrate then on my research. Her voice bathes the restaurant during orders. I don't see or hear David, but his work comes out in the messily wrapped paper, the grease seeping through, the smell of batter and canola oil. We all walk to the house at closing, around 9 p.m. David usually disappears inside. Sarah sometimes ends up driving me home because she's worried about me riding my bike in the dark or it is raining. We all seem comfortable in this pattern of Friday afternoons–into–evenings.

Dave says Sarah's a hoarder like her grandmother. She is always wearing brightly coloured vintage clothing, shiny dresses and floral skirts. Every outfit is a spectacle. I ask Dave if she's ever bought him anything and he screws up his nose and says he warned her off the first time when she bought a pair of blue hippie pants. Like fucking Byron Bay, he says, but his voice betrays a certain tenderness I've seen with the dog. I get a few lines out of him sometimes, but whenever I feel like I've made progress, he shuts off from me again.

On a quiet Friday night at the fish 'n' chip shop, Sarah comes over to my table and says she picked up a jacket for me at a Vinnies in Redcliffe.

'Me?'

'Yeah. It will suit you so much.' She smiles.

I don't wear jackets anymore, I don't wear much really.

I like the unisex university T-shirt and the cropped jeans I got in a sale. I don't pay much attention to clothes. One day Sarah said she liked the hoodie I was wearing. Dave said he liked it, too. It was one of those ones with a sporting team across the front. *Chicago Bears*. I don't know where I got it or what sport they play. I should have asked them.

We grow so comfortable in each other's presence, our Friday afternoon routine and phone calls during the week. I start to think what it means. A shaping of a sister-in-law, a dear friend, could this be part of the package of my life? I don't make friends like this. I smile thinking of her while working on the computer, transcribing recordings. If it is adoration it will be my own mistake.

She brought it up one afternoon, surprising me. She came up with the words. 'We have a strong bond, Jodie. It's hard to describe. It's quite special, and a gift. Overpowering at times. I don't want you to confuse it.'

We are out on the beach with Scary, low tide, shoes off, walking out through the shallows. Scary runs leadless to the grooves of water, licking the salt with delirium, and when satisfied it won't kill her, pushes her paws in with abandon, splashing mud droplets onto our clothes.

The sky is filled with red kites, kiteboarders in front of us. There are other dogs, which Scary treats with disdain. And couples with their kids. Scary likes people, especially children. Sarah's equally noticed by the children. They smile at her, and she talks to them. I'm amazed at her lack of pretension. I think, numbly, Sarah is a carer-type person. She will make a good mother.

We are quiet for a while as we walk. We walk right out. This is the ocean. Sarah scrubs her legs with grey sand, to exfoliate, she says. I copy her. It is only now, on the beach, I see she is beautiful. Radiant, even. And I wonder how I, and my brother, got into her life.

Her compliments flow quickly and easily. Don't tell me I'm a good person, I think. When all I want to do is complicate things, dirty your heart. I don't say anything, I just nod and she makes plans for a simple friendship. She talks as if it is easy. But I've mistimed love like stepping off a station platform and falling through the gap. Why now do I desire to have my breasts on hers?

'I've got some extra blueberries,' she says back at the house. 'Do you want to take some home?'

I put the punnet, chilled from the refrigerator, in my bicycle basket. When I get home, I open and light my unit, and get out a tub of plain yoghurt from the fridge and a white porcelain bowl. In the thick texture of the yoghurt the blueberries open up like stars. The fresh fruit stings my lips. I think about how I don't eat as much fruit as I should. I eat like a beggar when I'm not with her. She is a connoisseur and when we eat we eat like we're in love.

'David knows,' she says.

More often now, she is upset. She is upset, but she doesn't say it's because of David. I worry about her, make sure she's stocked up with boxes of water crackers and ginger ale for the nausea. I get her books out of the library. When we walk I hold Scary so she has her hands free and has her balance. Her backache is a fixture of my thoughts. I think

213

about taking a massage course advertised on the notice board on campus. Then, what to say to her? Can I massage you? Would you like a massage? Would she lie on her bed, take off her dress? This is all too much to think about.

There are rules to this. In this language, we don't say 'attraction'. We don't say 'sex'. We don't say 'love'.

The next time I see Sarah she opens the door already distracted, and says she's been crook, she hasn't made anything to eat. I ask her if Dave is home and she says he's gone out, and he wouldn't be working that night. David has started to take off a lot. I don't know where he goes. Sometimes it is for days at a time. He loads a backpack with his laptop and some clothes. A young man, he can go wherever he chooses. He has enough friends for us to wonder where he is. I don't know if he sees Michael and the others anymore. I do know he doesn't like to miss work; he needs the money.

'Is everything okay?' I ask.

'Yes,' she says.

'Do you know where he is?'

She shakes her head. I want to smooth the worry on her forehead.

'If you'd rather be alone, let me know,' I say with my hand leveraged on my hip. 'It's up to you.'

'No, stay,' she says. 'I'll make you something in a bit. First I want to show you …'

She presents to me the china cabinet of the grandmother who has recently died. I stand patiently and try not to fold my arms as she talks me through each piece, the year and where it was made, how much it was bought for, how much it's worth now. She shows me the bone china, pressing it up against the light of the pale ceiling bulb. We are close but not touching. There is something about the house – the old woman is still present, it is uneasy but also comforting. I feel she is sitting in the old armchair in the corner, her head against the neatly folded crocheted blanket on the top, her hands on the lap of a cherry-stained dress. Sarah taps me on the sleeve and asks if I want something to eat. She takes out crackers from the cupboard and I watch her smear over plant-based spread and then a thick layer of Vegemite. My mother force-fed me Vegemite when I was a child. I want to tell Sarah I don't like it but she's kind to think of me when she's sick and she's holding the cracker to my lips and I tell myself to think of something else as I open my mouth, embrace the scent of her buttered fingers and aniseed neck and I hardly taste the Vegemite. My body is heightened until she moves away, sweeping the crumbs off the bench and collecting them in her palm. She shuts the window against the wind. I don't want to be here when my brother gets home.

She goes into another room and brings me the jacket, a bright purple-blue blazer.

'Nice colour,' I say.

'Five dollars.' She smiles triumphantly. 'I'll get it dry-cleaned tomorrow and bring it over.'

'No, it's okay. '

'No, you're always coming over here, I'll get it to you easy.'

My throat tightens. I want to tell her the dry-clean

isn't as much as it's worth, but what is it worth in a dead hoarder's house? And what will she think of my flat – the pinpoints that show little more to my existence than my brother, offhand study, and her.

My tongue still tingling from the pretend taste of her, I leave fingerprint poetry on the door frame and stair railing as I leave. My heart is a black cat under a car. There is plenty left of the afternoon to wonder what I might have said. But there is tomorrow to ponder. The intensity of my feelings to be retained. The unknown fibres of my inner workings to be kept in a secure lab without sunlight.

My brother hits more when he drinks. My mother appeared those times with a bruised, yellow face. The scent of alcohol lingered on her, too. I can't look at my brother's eyes. I shut my eyes when he swings. I cry out. There is a song I hear in my mind when there is darkness. An old song that I have known since the beginning of my memory.

The windy morning before Sarah comes I take a vitamin C tablet, convinced it might stop me craving the orange of her skin. I wash it down with half a glass of water.

'You look well,' she says to me when she comes in. An easy thing to say, but still I smile.

'So do you,' I say.

'And you'll look even better in this jacket.' She holds it up, still in its plastic cover, then puts it down on the bench. She unzips the bag and I try the coat on for size. Drop it on my shoulders, do the only button up.

'It's not too tight around the bust?' she asks, in a low voice.

I shake my head, frightened to look up. Then I catch her eye when I do, and her hands come up as if she's going to touch me, but she lets them fall to her side. I wrestle the jacket off and put it back down on the bench.

'The fit's fine,' I say. 'Thank you.'

And then, the startling clarity of her hand on my waist, drawing me close, the intimacy of the half-embrace. We pull out and she looks back at me with a heavy expectancy. I have left the screen door open and the leaves blow up to the door. A thrilling spring sound. In not too long, she is where I have imagined her, my lips pointed at her. Five flickers of light before she kisses me, before I kiss her back. My body responds with a white pain, the type of pain you don't remember. We clutch, we claw each other. I trace my fingernails up the inside of her arm, and to the curve of her top lip. We take off our clothes until we're down to our underwear. I trip over the ankles of my jeans, curl them over my heels and leave them on the floor.

For those easy moments I haven't thought of David, but there it is, David and Sarah, David throwing bread, cutting holes in his flannelette shirt. Dave screaming at Sarah and her on the floor, hurt.

Her chest is in front of me. She breathes low. Her shaped stomach. Her firm arms. Her tight shoulders. The grainy exposure of her neck. My brother's lover. She moves my hand to her breasts, my brother's breasts. I trace the shape of them through her bra.

Unclothed we're on my bed, her knees at my armpits, her palms flat and open next to me. Her breasts are like lemons. Her skin bruises against mine. She curls her fingers closer to the need of me, her soft thigh presses against mine. I gasp as she moves, she circles me and her mouth moves to my breast. She sucks it with the same rhythm and at the feel of her teeth I feel myself close and groan out. She moves downward with her mouth, and with her tongue she makes me come, wonderfully, feverishly, and I'm feeble after that, but not enough to stop me wanting her, wanting to make her sigh, and I gravitate to her, moving on top and pressing into her. She is deliciously wet, and I put my hand in between us. It is only a short moment until she joins me, shouting, sighing. I kiss her deeply and see how relaxed she looks, eyes curled up. I think of the baby inside her, resting. I want to place my hand on her stomach but instead I take in her form, not trusting myself with words.

When we get up my flat is not the same. Every inch of the floorplan projects a freeze frame of our physicality. When she leaves I feel her kiss dry off my lips, her saliva evaporate from my thighs. Only the furniture is visibly shifted, the lounge on an angle, the bed half a metre off the wall.

The door closes and she is gone for twenty hours.

A woman I met once had been on a program to quit smoking. They told her how she would feel when she regained her normal sense of smell and taste, peeling an orange. A week later she'd kicked the urge, and the navel orange underneath her fingernails was the most powerful sensation she'd had in her life. When I asked her if it was the anticipation, she thought about it and nodded.

Sarah has talked to me about names for the baby, if it's a girl. She says she still has a baby names book she got from Lifeline when she was ten. Her grandmother used to take her to the vintage stores on the north side, and Sarah would go sit by the books. Her grandmother didn't want her to buy it, no doubt thinking about a teenage pregnancy, but Sarah convinced her and the book remains on the bookshelf. She has had many favourite names, but there are a few that have endured. She likes names that are hardy, shapely, circular. Old-fashioned but other-worldly. She likes Grete, Lachina and Margo. I tell her I like Grete the best, that it reminds me of a warrior's name. This child, I say, if she is a girl, will be a strong girl, like her mother. I ask Sarah if Dave has names he likes; have they talked about it? She says he wants a name that doesn't look like anything else.

'Is he back?' is the first thing I ask Sarah when she's at my door the next morning.

'Yes,' she says softly. She has let her hair out and pulls a piece in front of her mouth, hiding it, keeping it from me.

I hastily move to grab a chair with a thick cushion on the back for her and we sit down, facing each other. 'Where was he?'

'He didn't tell me.'

'You said he knew about ...' I am anxious. 'About this. Us.'

'Some of it. I told him we'd talked about a connection. He himself thought it was strange, and had noticed it. Maybe feels left out. But, Jodie, he can never find out about this.'

'What are we going to do?'

'I don't know,' she says. 'The nausea has been bad lately. I can't cook.'

I touch her shoulder. 'Sarah, you know he has a mental illness.'

She moves my hand away and I feel the loss. 'He's just having a rough time. With your mum, and everything that happened. Your dad dying. He's a twenty-year-old; he doesn't have things figured yet. He has a bit of a temper. But he's not crazy.'

'Sarah, did he tell you he spent a few weeks in the mental health ward of the hospital? Did he tell you what happened when he left? Why he didn't finish school?'

'I'm looking after him,' she says.

'You got to look after yourself, too.'

She starts to get up, holding her stomach.

'Has he hurt you?'

She won't answer. Then, 'Jodie, why are you doing this?'

'I just want to protect you,' I say. 'He's living with you, and I worry. What he might do to you. All I've ever wanted is to protect you.'

'I don't need that,' Sarah says. 'Maybe you should have been thinking about your brother.'

'I do think about him! Every day. Sarah, I've tried and tried and tried. But he's a danger to others.'

After she leaves I know I've said too much, that I have loved wrongly.

When Dave was in the hospital I remember going to the ward for a visit. There was a courtyard with palm trees and

Dave sat there with me. The other patients would come past and acknowledge him, but he wouldn't say anything. He had marks up his arms and looked so thin. We both sat there in silence. I waited for him to say sorry. I waited to say sorry. The doctor came by, well dressed in her jacket and pencil skirt, and said he would not be allowed to leave, they would prevent him from leaving until they thought he was ready. When we met alone, she asked me why my mother didn't know yet. I said that I would tell my mother. The doctor told me the name of the medication he was on. The side-effects, and how they were monitoring it. 'Is he normally like this?' she asked. I answered as best I could and she went away. I sat next to my brother again. I had brought him a packed bag of clothes and toiletries. We looked at the sky, faded red from an afternoon storm. A breeze spun through the gap between the buildings. My brother looked at me and smiled, he said they had turtles here and for that second, that moment, I thought he was getting better. Hope for him. Hope for me.

I keep my distance from the house, from Sarah and David. I tell myself it's best for all of us, that Sarah doesn't want to see me anymore. I must only remember how upset she is with me. I can't think of her skin against mine. It has been two weeks. I have met my supervisor and there is a lot of work to be done between now and November, but I spend a fair bit of time staring out of my balcony or lying in bed. At night I listen to the radio – no music – the news channel, so there is always talking. I sob after I touch myself, a tangle of sheets around my ankles. A grieving that is not dignified, nor quiet.

Sarah told me about the first time she saw me come in to the fish shop. She said she knew immediately I was David's sister, how could I not be? We have the same face. She said she was filled with a warmth at discovering this, that I was a person that could easily enter into her life. She had found out she was pregnant that day, at the doctor's in Chermside.

I think about going to the animal park in Dakabin and watching the turtles, watching them swim and also lie on the rocks. I hope they have real rocks there.

One night, late, I wake up to a message from Sarah on my phone. She can't stop thinking about me. About the day we were together. She wants to be in my arms. She wants my hands on her breasts. I go to the kitchen and have a glass of wine before I reply.

There is a movie on television, a space one. David used to love the *Star Wars* movies, and he got books of the series out of the library. He would insist on reading out loud from them. He would do it on long car trips when Dad was trying to find us somewhere to live, running from the loan sharks.

Sarah tells me she and Dave have had a blue and he's left again. I fill another wine glass. Outside, a bat flaps over the park. My legs are shaking. My phone beeps a few times an hour. In this blue room of technological seduction we tell each other things that should be physical. We are in love with each other. It is just no good not to be together. I tell her to come over, I want her here. And she doesn't respond; my phone sits in self-imposed darkness.

★

Let me not forget that our mother used to hit us, too. That my little brother would cry at the first violation of child's flesh, a mother's touch turned untoward. These tears would suspend from his puffed round eyes and go nowhere. His body was so close to mine as we took shelter in the bathroom of our house, standing in the bathtub with the pale yellow curtain closed. Together, refugees, but we were not one. We could not look at each other. The saltiness of her wild, primal screams still on our mouths. I did not tell my little brother I would take him away from it. That I would protect him, that I would stand up to her. It was not in my capacity.

I said I'd keep my distance but a couple of times I go to Sandgate and just walk around, spying from the fringes. On a cloudy day, I walk on the path beside the beach, starting at the playground, past the pool and the cafe across from it. I don't see her.

As I look out into the ocean I remember my brother's grip on the back of my head, pulling my hair as the sea water plunged into my throat, a scream underwater. Back then, I was bigger, but only just. A couple of kicks and he'd let me go.

I go over to the Sandgate home by bus – my tyres are low. The sticky flowers from the yellow trees are peeled over the footpath. Dave is shirtless in the front yard moving stuff in a wheelbarrow. His chest and shoulders are pale against the rest of his body. I have pulled the blue-purple jacket over a black T-shirt dress with tights, and when I see his outfit, I realise the foolishness of mine; it will be a thirty-five degree day and I have sweated just walking from the bus stop. I clip open the gate and Dave looks up.

'She's not here,' he says.

'Where is she?' I say, moving closer.

'At the shops, I think.'

'How are you going?'

'Fine. Hey, sis, did you ever see a shovel round here, by any chance?'

I shake my head.

He sifts through another large plastic tub.

'I want you to stay away from her,' he says. His eyes cold.

'What do you mean? Sarah?'

'I've seen the messages. I know all of it.' He is smiling, unnervingly.

I don't know what to make of it, his stance is not threatening.

'Now,' he says. 'Will you help me find a shovel?'

I follow him, under the house. I now see the extent of Sarah's grandmother's collecting. She has left boxes and furniture in every corner of the dirt boxroom. I pull things aside productively, because I haven't seen David this agitated for a while. Since he's been here, maybe. It is as if I had forgotten this side of him, but of course I hadn't, this is what I had worried about the whole time. It is almost a relief that there is no pretence about it. There is me and him and his shoulders square as he grunts in frustration.

'I'm going to get something upstairs,' he says. 'Wait here.'

I step towards the door to watch him go up the back steps. He takes the steps two at a time, holding a screwdriver in his hand. I see the dog's bed, an old hessian bag, she has scratched the corners of it. Next to the bed, Scary's stainless steel drinking bowl is dry, a layer of green mould at the bottom. I wonder how long Sarah has been out.

The backyard is also painted with the gold flowers. Seedpods from a neighbouring tree collect under the clothesline. When I walk back out into the yard there is something to the left of my vision that I didn't see when I was indoors.

I see the dried blood on the concrete and the swarming flies. A tennis ball, open, still. Scary is on the ground on her side, irreversibly dead. Blood everywhere.

Directly above me in the house are my brother's footsteps, pressing against the floorboards. His heels touch before his toes. I keep my eyes half-shut and my hands around my cheeks as I turn to walk out of there, back onto the street before he notices. The gate creaks when I touch it, and I can't find the energy to pull it shut.

Acknowledgements

Thank you to these people and more. My family – particularly my parents, for their support. Bec Jessen, who has been there for every step. Sue Abbey, for her belief in me. Melissa Lucashenko, Krissy Kneen, Inga Simpson and Sharon Phillips for reading and encouraging.

This started from a little story ('S&J') – that got published in a big journal (*McSweeney's*) – thanks Chris Flynn and Jordan Bass for seeing something in my writing. Judith Lukin-Amundsen, for her editorial insight and reassurance. Everyone at UQP, in particular, Madonna Duffy and Jacqueline Blanchard. And the Queensland Literary Awards, for continuing the David Unaipon Award.

Stories from this collection have appeared in the following journals:

McSweeney's Issue 41, (July 2012) and *The Best of McSweeney's* (December 2013) 'S&J'.

Ora Nui Special Edition: A Collection of Maori and Aboriginal Literature (2013) 'Hot Stones'.

CPSIA information can be obtained
at www.ICGtesting.com
Printed in the USA
FFOW01n0235081015
17411FF